# HELL PASS

The circus comes to the town of Angel Pass, but does it bring simple pleasure for the hard-working cowboys and wide-eyed children of the community — or something more sinister? Fresh from a mission to discover the fate of his lovely partner's long lost brother and faced with a series of bizarre kidnappings and jewel robberies, ex-manhunter Hannigan endeavours to find out. But will the secrets of the past prove more disturbing than the revelations of the present?

LANCE HOWARD

◆

# HELL PASS

*Complete and Unabridged*

**LINFORD**
*Leicester*

First published in Great Britain in 2007 by
Robert Hale Limited
London

First Linford Edition
published 2008
by arrangement with
Robert Hale Limited
London

The moral right of the author has been asserted

British Library CIP Data

Howard, Lance
    Hell Pass.—Large print ed.—
Linford western library
1. Western stories
2. Large type books
I. Title
823.9′14 [F]

ISBN 978–1–84782–281–9

Published by
F. A. Thorpe (Publishing)
Anstey, Leicestershire

Set by Words & Graphics Ltd.
Anstey, Leicestershire
Printed and bound in Great Britain by
T. J. International Ltd., Padstow, Cornwall

This book is printed on acid-free paper

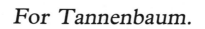

*For Tannenbaum.*

# 1

Five riders gouged spurs into their horses' flanks, driving the animals to speeds greater than they normally would have dared. A stumble, a broken ankle, and any one of them might never see his grim mission through to completion.

A mission upon which a child's life depended.

Looks of fury mingled with dread strained the men's faces. Wild-eyed, cheeks flushed with crimson, they gritted their teeth and took their chances with the horses' welfare as well as their own, because even a minute lost might doom their task to failure.

Hoofbeats drummed like Gatling fire. Dust billowed in gritty clouds that choked their nostrils, stung their eyes and coated their flapping dusters. Autumn air slapped at their clothing and bit into their bare hands, which were bleached and aching from clenching the reins too tightly.

The scent of death pervaded the air, decaying leaves, possibly, the fate of the innocent, certainly.

In the distance a great swirl of dust clouded the trail; it hovered on the horizon, marking the passage of the quarry these men sought. Far off, shouts and curses from wagon drivers punctuated the early-afternoon air. Clattering iron tires and creaking springs signaled the hurried departure of the death caravan now less than a mile ahead.

The riders had made good time; it wouldn't take long to overtake the circus crew who'd departed Tarrowville a half-hour before.

At the sight of the wagons the riders spurred their mounts' sides without mercy. The target was in sight; that was all that mattered. Huge muscles rippling, quivering, the horses snorted and neighed. Steam blew from their nostrils;

slobber streamed from their mouths.

The distance narrowed.

Anticipation replaced some of the dread and anger on the riders' faces. Those sons-of-bitches would soon pay for their crime; that was at least a measure of comfort.

Hills and jutting ledges rose to either side of the trail. Stands of fir, spruce and pine blanketed the steep inclines; boulders and jagged slabs of stone peppered the landscape. Aspen and ash, maple and cottonwood displayed a dazzling panorama of gold and red and flame-orange. Somewhere a bobcat screamed, the sound unnerving to two men who watched the proceedings, apprehension stiffening their carriages and pinching their faces.

High above the trail, a half-mile ahead of the riders, the two men poised atop their mounts on an open patch of ground.

They peered down, gazes jumping from the circus train in the distance to the riders charging hell-bent along the trail.

The first man's lips drew tight and his dark eye narrowed. Worry danced in his nerves, an emotion he seldom allowed himself to indulge. A young man, just shy of his mid-twenties, his longish black hair danced in the breeze and flittered across his forehead. His skin carried an olive complexion that hinted at a mixed Mexican heritage. He wore no hat and a patch covered his left eye. A scar snaked from his temple to his cheek and a thick black beard peppered with early signs of gray covered a strong chin. His clothing, a billowy shirt, tight trousers and high boots, pegged him as belonging to the circus caravan on the trail below.

Rajas Vago owned that circus, but more importantly he was responsible for its secrets — secrets he had no intention or desire to share with the riders chasing it down. Secrets that were surely enough to get a man buried.

'This is goddamned bad news.' The man beside Vago shook his head, then

4

spat. He was shorter than Vago, five-foot-ten at the most, stockier, with dark hair, olive skin and the look of an animal backed into a corner. A loose silk shirt stitched with sequins covered his barrel chest; tan trousers fit like a second skin on his thick legs and shiny black boots came to his knees. A jeweled dagger rested in a sheath at either side of his waist. The Devil lived in his dark eyes and whereas Rajas Vago had become practiced at hiding his true nature, Avara Ganado wore his sin like a badge of honor.

'I count five,' Vago said in a matter-of-fact tone that said he was stating the obvious more to calm his nerves than for Ganado's benefit. His lanky frame shifted in the saddle.

Ganado's brow cinched. 'Christ, I told you we were pushing our luck, Alejandro — '

'You know goddamn better'n to call me that!' Vago's head spun, eye glaring, fury sweeping across his features. 'You make that mistake again and I'll hand you over to those men riding our ass.'

Ganado's teeth came together and his eyes narrowed a fraction, but he apparently thought better of challenging Vago.

'Just sayin' we did it too close together this time. One town, then the next a few days later. Folks were bound to get suspicious.'

'They don't know anything for certain. They're guessing.' Vago's gaze dropped, focusing on the riders again.

'They find out what's in that wagon and our necks will get a hell of a lot longer. Stoled loot's one thing, but chil — '

'I know, goddammit!' Vago's voice snapped like a gunshot and his hands tightened on the bay's reins. He glanced at the Winchester in its saddle-boot, then the Smith & Wesson at his hip. Wholesale murder wasn't normally on their itinerary but he couldn't allow those riders to make a discovery that would send them to the gallows. Ganado was right: he *had* risked the

6

operation by planning two towns so close together, with a third on the horizon. He shuddered, teeth clenched. Controlling the darkness lurking within him was getting more difficult and it sent anger sizzling through his veins. If he lost his hold over the blackness in his soul, he lost his strength. He refused to let that happen. Within Rajas Vago was no room for weakness, not ever again. No one would ever take what was his. No one would prevent him from taking what he wanted, needed, would kill for.

Rage exploded over him, making his hands shake on the reins and his fingernails gouge into his palms. 'God-damn them . . . ' he mumbled, then grabbed the Winchester from its saddle-boot and jammed the butt to his shoulder. He levered shells and fired twice, the report startling Ganado half-out of his saddle. The recoil sent welts of pain through Vago's shoulder and down his arm, pain he barely noticed.

'What the hell are you doing?'

shouted Ganado, face painted in shock. 'You can't hit them from here, you damn fool! You'll just warn them we're layin' an ambush.'

Vago stared at the riders as they hurtled forward, all of them intact. He'd likely missed by yards, but had gotten lucky, because the pounding of their horses' hoofs had drowned out the thunder of the shots.

Vago shuddered with a fury-driven tremor that gripped his entire frame. Sweat sprang out on his forehead. 'Jesus . . . ' he muttered, belly cinching. What the hell had come over him? He'd ordered the caravan to ride ahead on the notion they might have aroused the town's suspicions and he had nearly thrown away the element of surprise.

Vago shoved the rifle into the saddleboot, then peered at Ganado. 'You know what we gotta do.'

Ganado nodded. 'I know, but five men ain't gonna be as easy as taking one — '

'Sure it will. They won't be expecting

us and we'll be on them before they know it.'

Vago heeled his horse into motion, taking the incline at an angle with less caution than would have been advisable under normal circumstances. But he saw little choice. If the men got too far ahead, caught up with the wagon train, they might take casualties.

Behind him, Ganado descended, only slightly more wary of having his horse misstep and go tumbling down the hill.

They reached the trail, the dust from the five riders' passage still clouding the air. Vago heeled his horse into a gallop, Ganado following suit, a few beats behind.

The riders had caught up to the caravan. The ornate wagons weren't built for speed; the pace at which they now traveled in an attempt to outrun their pursuers jeopardized axles and draught horses alike. The paneled wagons, ten of them, rattled and clanged. Shouts and curses from drivers and circus performers blistered the air.

A gunshot crashed out, coming from one of the performers, a woman dressed in gypsy fashion who wielded an old Sharps. The murderous glee on her face belied the perilous situation.

The wagon train was little more than a sitting duck to the riders, all of whom now had their guns out and were angling to either side of the caravan. Shots stuttered out; lead chipped paint and splinters from the vehicles. The gypsy withdrew like a rabbit darting into a hole when a bullet plowed into the wagon an inch from her dark-haired head. The side of the wagon proclaimed the legend: Madam Mystique, Seer of All, but apparently she had not divined the bullet with her name on it. Only through stroke of luck and jouncing carriage did she escape certain death.

The riders aimed for a particular wagon, a drab paneled box of a vehicle third in line. Its sides bare of legend, it appeared merely an equipment carrier.

More shots thundered, a few other performers deciding to try their luck or test fate. One, a willowy fellow dressed as a ringmaster, aimed a derringer at one rider who had come nearly even with his wagon. The wagon took a jump as an iron tire bounced over a sizable stone and so did the ringmaster's gun hand. The derringer went off, accidentally discharging both its bullets. Neither hit the target, but the rider's face contorted in fury and he blasted a shot that plucked the ringmaster half out of his seat. The willowy man seemed suspended in air an instant, shock on his face, blood spreading like a death rose across his boiled shirt. The rider triggered another shot and the man slammed against the front of the wagon, then bounced forward, falling amongst horses' traces. Hoofs pounded his head and bones to a bloody mess and an iron tire nearly took it clean off his body. The rider turned away, unable to watch the gruesome end of his attacker.

The second man sitting in the driver's seat struggled with the reins, having no desire to test his shooting skill and every intention to stop the horses from careening whichever way they wanted, having been spooked by the shot and the trampled ringmaster. The rider shouted at the man to stop the wagon, leveled his gun on the fellow as an encouragement, but the driver was either too terrified or too stupid to obey.

The rider prepared to blast the driver out of his seat, but another shot rang out from behind him. He jerked bolt upright in the saddle, his entire frame stiffening, a bullet punching out the front of his shirt. Blood trickled from his mouth and his hands went slack on the reins. He toppled off the horse, foot jerking from its boot, which caught in the stirrup. Body hitting the hardpack, he tumbled over and over, rolling to stop alongside the trail, unmoving. His horse charged on, directionless.

Glancing at the fallen rider, Rajas Vago let a satisfied grin cross his lips, the gun still smoking in his hand. 'One down . . . ' he muttered, gaze jumping back to the task at hand, the four remaining riders.

With Vago's killing of their comrade, the other four became aware of the two men charging at them from the rear. The element of surprise vanished and all that remained was to fight.

Riders broke rank, angling around and back in an effort to confront the new threat. Forgotten in the reality of a more dangerous adversary, the wagon train plowed forward, scattered shots winging back, none doing any damage other than to kick up chunks of trail dirt and clouds of dust.

A bullet whizzed past Vago; he jerked the reins left. The horse bucked in its step, nearly throwing him, but he managed to hold on and avoid the lead meant for his heart.

Ganado fired from the right, a rapid shot that came more from frantic nerves than skill. He got lucky. One of the riders hurtled backwards off his horse and landed flat on his back on the trail, a bullet in his shoulder. He struggled to get to his feet, one hand still clamped to his Colt.

'None of that . . . ' Vago whispered, drawing a bead on the man. One shot. The man's brains spattered the hardpack.

'Hah!' shouted Vago, sending his horse careening at the three remaining riders. To the right, Ganado did the same.

The riders appeared suddenly confused, worried, obviously not having expected a surprise attack or this much resistance from the circus caravan. If Vago had made mistakes, then these men had errored worse, and fatally. He couldn't have guessed just what they had anticipated from the band, but they had seriously misjudged their adversary.

They would pay for that mistake with their lives.

Shots thundered through the air, coming from both riders and carnies.

A lucky shot from the gypsy plucked the hat from one of the riders, who

14

spun in an effort to return the favor.

Ganado, aiming a bit more carefully this time, blasted the rider from his horse. The man hit the ground to the side of the trail, lay groaning, and Ganado put another shot into his chest, silencing him for good.

The two remaining riders coddled thoughts of retreat; it showed plain on their faces. Self-preservation was a powerful force. Their ranks decimated, their confidence and anger dissolved, their only thoughts likely focused on escape and forming a posse to run down their quarry at a later date. The innocent life that chanced being lost . . . well, guilt could be dealt with later.

Vago refused to give them that chance. He triggered more shots, keeping his horse dancing left, then right to make himself less of a target. Even so, a bullet tore a streak across his cheek; blood dribbled into his beard.

He retaliated, blasting two quick shots. A bullet took a rider in the neck, kicking him off his mount and leaving him gurgling in the dust. It wouldn't be long before the life ran out of him, so Vago ignored the spasming body.

He reined up, focus locking on the remaining rider, who also drew to a halt.

Vago squeezed the trigger again, aim locked on the last man. An empty clack sounded. Christ, he was out of bullets.

The rider's face washed from fear to relief to spite. His gun came up, centered on the one-eyed circus owner.

'Goddamn you, Vago!' the rider yelled, finger tightening on the trigger.

Two shots came, one a heartbeat behind the other. Ganado had fired first, putting a bullet through the rider's head. The second shot came from the rider's gun, as his finger reflexively spasmed on the trigger.

The bullet nearly took off a piece of Vago's ear.

The rider toppled off his horse, hit the hardpack with a thud and lay still.

Vago stared a moment, breath beating out in fiery gasps, sweat pouring down his face, mingling with the blood from the graze on his cheek.

Ahead the circus train slowed to halt, awaiting their return.

Ganado angled his mount up beside Vago. 'We got goddamn lucky that time. We best skip the next town before — '

'No!' Vago snapped, with a violent shake of his head. 'We go on as planned.'

'Goddammit, Rajas, there might be more where those men came from. They catch up to us and maybe it will be with a posse next time. We can't risk it.'

'Angel Pass is far enough away. We'll take our chances.'

Ganado stared at Vago for long moments, his dark face fraught with doubt and a look that asked if Vago had just plain lost his mind. 'You got some other reason why that town's so damned important?'

Vago almost smiled. Ganado was getting too smart for his own good. 'What reason would I have? Same as all the rest of these towns.'

Doubt flashed across Ganado's features. 'Yeah? I've seen the look in your eye every time someone mentions that town. And I know you were sneaking off for some reason. I saw some cowboy passing you information, too. You wanna tell me what's there that's got you so fired up?'

'Maybe I'll tell you when we reach it. For now, all you need to know is I got a mission there . . . one I've waited too many years to complete.'

'We're taking too many chances. Maybe we should just ride out after you finish whatever it is you got to do.'

'And pass up an opportunity for ripe pickings? Not a chance.'

Ganado glanced at the carnage on the trail about them, the apprehension on his face strengthening. 'Angel Pass ain't a welcoming place for the likes of us, Vago.'

'No? Seems appropriate to me.'

'What the hell does that mean?'

Vago uttered a laugh that seemed

somehow detached. 'It's ironic, really. Because for once in my life I aim to see God's wrath brought to two folks who live there . . . I aim to give the 'angels' a vision of Hell . . . '

# 2

'Careful, you'll fall in!' shouted the little boy, shaking a finger at the younger dark-haired girl sitting on the bank of the river, struggling with a fishing pole he'd whittled for her from a branch. 'Tooties don't float, you nincompoop!' Alejandro del Pelado said it with a grin and fought to keep his own pole from being jerked into the rushing water.

'Don't call me that, you ninny!' the five-year-old shouted back, hands bone-white on the pole, small muscles quivering. Her high-laced shoes dug into the soft ground, as she fought with whatever had gobbled the bait on the end of her pole. Sweat sprang out on her forehead and the French braids to either side of her face bobbed. Gritting her teeth, she gave the battle a mighty effort but was leaning too far forward and in danger of losing what was likely a large trout or catfish.

Her brother laughed and it annoyed her. He didn't think she could do it, no matter what he had told their parents when he convinced them to let him take her out fishing. She suspected her parents had relented more out of the need to escape her constant babbling questions, than out of any conviction she had reached the proper age to contribute to the family's food supply.

'You're gonna fall in,' Alejandro repeated, his features a little more strained now as he dug in his heels and fought to bring in the prize at the end of his own line.

'I won't either!' she shouted, but secretly worried she just might go tumbling into the river. Her arms ached and her legs shook from the strain.

Her name was Angela del Pelado, but Alejandro tormented her with the nickname Tootie for the very reason her parents had let her accompany her older brother, who was just a shade past his ninth birthday. She never stopped talking, the way little girls were wont to do. But so many questions filled her mind and they bubbled out like the rushing waters of the river. Sometimes she thought she might burst with them. 'Toot, toot, never mute,' Alejandro constantly teased.

But she couldn't stay mad at him. He watched out for her, protected her from some of the other children who hated her Mexican-white mix. Last week three boys at the schoolhouse had thrown her in a mud puddle, soiling her new Easter dress. They would have destroyed it completely had Alejandro not chased them off. He was her guardian angel, she reckoned.

But he did prickle her sometimes.

A sudden jerk snapped her reverie and she couldn't stop herself from hurtling forward. Her knees buckled and the pole slipped through her hands with a burning welt of pain across both palms. A chopped scream escaped her lips and Alejandro let go of his own pole, making a grab for her as she flew face-first into the river.

She couldn't swim. She hadn't learned yet. Alejandro was supposed to teach her but she had been too scared of the water and resisted the lessons.

Ice water stung her face. The early-spring river had barely unfrozen and it wouldn't take long before her whole body went numb.

She went under, water flooding her mouth and throat before she had a chance to catch a breath and hold it. She tumbled forward, battered by the current, gathering speed. Kicking out with all her might, her head broke the surface and she coughed a great spray of river water, but couldn't catch a breath before sinking again.

Panic seized her. She couldn't scream, couldn't fight the torrent. Arms and legs flailing, she couldn't slow her forward plunge. The current tore her along, and any thoughts of the fish at the end of her pole and how proud she would have been to show her ma and pa she was a big girl were swept away with it.

Rocks loomed ahead. That thought rose unbidden in her mind, accompanied by a new surge of panic. If she hit those jagged stones it wouldn't matter how much water she swallowed; she'd be crushed against them.

Pain spiked her chest and lungs, but now, oddly, the water felt syrupy warm, strangely comforting. She didn't know why, or care, but wanted to give herself over to the sensation. The edges of her mind grew fuzzy, glowing.

★   ★   ★

'Tootie!' Running along the shore, Alejandro screamed his sister's name over and over, seeing her small form bob above the water for a moment then disappear back under. Terror made his heart pound, rose beads of sweat on his forehead, despite the chill in the air.

'Tootie, no!' He darted along the shore, kicking off his shoes, then flinging his jacket to the ground. He saw the rocks jutting from the water a hundred feet downstream, knew if she hit those he'd have no chance to save her.

Judging how far his sister had traveled since she last went under, he hurled himself into the water. Its icy arms embraced him, shocked him, tried to whisk him forward. He was a strong swimmer, having fallen into the river a few times on his lonesome, though he would never have admitted that to Tootie, but the current was nearly overpowering.

His arms knifed into the water, feet thrusting, cutting diagonally across the current. Already breath burned in his lungs, and his muscles trembled with exertion.

With every ounce of his strength, he stroked onward. She had submerged about twenty yards back and with the speed at which the water was traveling, she should be just about —

He dove, the chill stinging his face,

shocking his open eyes. The world beneath the stream appeared a blurry, foreign realm, filled with flashing images of indistinct objects, likely fish and grass uprooted by the torrent and whisked along. He glimpsed a flash of white, knew that had to be Tootie's dress, the old one she wore for traipsing through the woods with him.

Thrusting out a hand, his fingers gripped fabric and a surge of relief rushed through to him.

With all his strength he kicked towards her, yanking the handful of material to him at the same time.

She was limp, and the river fought to tear her from his grasp, but through some grace of the Almighty Preacher Robbins went on about every Sunday when his parents dragged them to the Methodist church, he managed to draw her to his breast and clamp an arm about her fragile body.

His lungs ached powerfully and numbness tingled through his limbs. How long had he been under? Probably not longer than a minute, though panic exaggerated the time, but Tootie had been under longer, so he had precious few moments to get her to the surface before her lungs filled with water.

Teeth clamped, he thrust his legs downward with all his power. Up they came, breaking the surface in a great geyser of spray and streaming water.

He let out a yell, mostly from fear, but it gave him a burst of strength. Arm wrapped around her chest, he dragged her through the water towards the shore. Choking and coughing came from the little girl and relief surged through him, adding to his determination and strength.

A panorama of water and trees and threateningly close rocks, swept across his vision. His legs were weakening, filling with lead. The muscles in his arms quivered. He wouldn't last much longer, and Tootie, soaked, weighed double her weight.

Just a little farther, he told himself. Just a little farther. The shore was only a few yards away.

With a yell he gave it everything he had left. His kicking feet suddenly hit land and knew he had made it. A bit farther and he was able to stand, drag her onto the shore and lay her in the grass.

The little girl coughed and sputtered, spitting up more water than he would have thought possible for anyone to swallow. But she was alive and for that he thanked the invisible God the pastor was so fond of. Maybe He existed after all and wasn't just some mythical being like that Christmas fella who never seemed to find the del Pelado homestead the way he found other kids' homes.

'Tootie, are you OK?' he blurted, nearly with a burst of tears. He couldn't let her see him cry or he'd never hear the end of it.

She struggled to sit up, black hair plastered to her head, dress soaked and water dripping down her face. 'You . . . you nincompoop!' she yelled, and he was never so happy to be called a bad name. 'You let me fall in!'

In his relief he hugged her and laughed.

'I told you, Tooties don't float, silly girl . . . '

★ ★ ★

'Tooties don't float . . . ' the young woman on horseback whispered, coming from her reverie, gaze focused on the river far in the distance. Dressed in a low-pulled flat Mexican hat, errant strands of blue-black locks to either side of her Mex-spiced face riffling in the breeze, white blouse and riding skirt, she drew a composing breath and let it trickle out.

Angela del Pelado swallowed against the emotion cinching her throat as the memory drifted back to her. That long-ago day hadn't been her most celebrated; she'd nearly drowned. Even so, it unearthed a melancholy longing within her being, and brought a ghost of a smile to her full lips. It made her miss Alejandro all the more.

That day seemed a lifetime ago. A time before her parents' murders at the hands of brutal outlaws, before she was shipped off to the home by her aunt and uncle for being too wild, too grief-stricken. What the hell did they expect from a six-year-old girl who'd lost all sense of foundation, all that grounded her young life? She wasn't ready for the brutal realities of adulthood, but those lowly bastards who killed her parents had forced it upon her and her kin had dealt with the aftermath no better than she.

They had severed the remaining tether to her former life, by sending her away, separating her from Alejandro. She recollected him now in only vague flashes of memory, feelings burdened by sadness. She remembered him taking their parents' deaths sullenly, wallowing in despair and dark moments where even at her young age she had worried, over-worried, he might leave her permanently. He had talked almost lovingly about the river, its rushing waters, as if he had planned to throw himself in. The only thing that stopped him was her, and she knew that. But what became of him after she was sent away?

Her aunt and uncle had kept him, as best she knew, but by the time she left the home as a teen and tried to track down her kin they had vanished into the Colorado wilderness. She had searched, searched for years, in fact, but found no trace of them, no clue to their fate.

Until two weeks ago, when Jim Hannigan had taken it upon himself to use his Pinkerton contact and all his resources to track down Agnes and Harker Pendelton, her aunt and uncle, after she had told him of her early life in a moment of weakness. Or perhaps a moment of love; there was a thin line between the two. And bless him, he had acted, without her knowledge and with a great deal of hard work and cash to put into her lap the one thing he reckoned she wanted most.

He was wrong. What she wanted most was him, a life together. She wanted him to make love to her, share his secrets, too.

But the whereabouts of her brother came in a close second and she was indebted to Jim Hannigan for accomplishing what she hadn't been able to on her own.

Two weeks. That's how long it had taken her to gather the courage to confront her aunt and uncle and question them about her brother. She harbored little emotion for them one way or the other, having released her hate and anger years back for what they did to that six-year-old girl. She might never completely forgive them for separating her from Alejandro, but what good was holding onto rage? None. What's done was done. The only thing that mattered now was finding him, or discovering his fate.

Heart stepping up a beat, she

surveyed the landscape, the small cabin a few hundred yards ahead appearing so serene, its scattering of outbuildings suggesting an operation of modest means. Rolling hills surrounded the spread and its unassuming homestead. The entire compound appeared unobtrusive, nothing to single it out from any of a hundred other such places. As if someone had designed it that way on purpose. Someone who didn't want to be bothered. Someone who didn't want to be found.

She drew another calming breath, palms growing damp. Coming here was more difficult than she thought it would be.

*This is what you wanted, isn't it, Angela? This is what you waited years to find. What's holding you back now?*

The thought that he might be dead, she reckoned. She didn't care much what her aunt or uncle might say to her but the thought of what might have become of her brother brought a gnawing fear to her belly.

*Tooties don't float* . . .

She couldn't let herself dwell on the worst. For all she knew Alejandro was there with them, though Hannigan's research suggested that was not the case. What would she say to him if he were? Would he recognize her?

So many years. So many memories. So many disappointments.

'It's now or never, Tootie . . . ' she whispered, then gigged her horse into an easy gait towards the house.

Smoke curled from the chimney and the air was musky with the scent of old leaves and singed wood. The sun hovered just above the distant mountains and somehow everything appeared darker than it really was.

Reaching the house, she swung from the saddle and tethered the bay to the hitch post. Her legs shook a bit as she climbed the steps and crossed the creaking porch boards. Hesitating outside the door, she drew a deep breath, then rapped lightly on the wood.

Her heart jumped into her throat as

footsteps came from within, then a bolt drew back. The door opened and an older woman stared at her, a look of sudden recognition jumping onto her features. The woman tried to slam the door shut, but Tootie shoved a foot between the door and jamb and slapped a palm against the panel.

Tootie's features hardened. 'Oh, no, you don't. I've come too far to have the door slammed in my face.'

The older woman backed away and Tootie stepped inside, swinging the door shut behind her. The parlor interior was dingy, containing only a threadbare sofa, small table and a cedar chest by the window for furniture. She peered at the woman, startled at how old and haggard Agnes now appeared. Deep lines creased her forehead and dark pouches nested beneath her mouse-colored eyes. Her gray hair, thin and patchy, was pulled tight into a severe bun. A worn apron and drab dress hung loose on her skeletal frame. The years hadn't been kind, and Tootie almost felt sorry for her.

'What do you want?' Her aunt's voice came brittle, irritated.

'You recognize me?' Tootie struggled to make her heart stop pounding. Facing Agnes was harder than she had thought it would be. It unearthed old hurts and pain she thought she'd long ago sent packing. She reckoned she'd rather have stared down an outlaw.

The older woman's face pinched with a look that made her position on Tootie's finding her after all these years clear: Angela del Pelado was unwelcome, an intruder. 'I do . . . you haven't changed that much.'

Tootie offered a fragile smile. 'I didn't rightly expect a warm welcome but didn't figure on the door being slammed in my face, either.' Tootie wrapped her arms about herself, suppressing the urge to tremble from nerves.

The old woman's face hardened another notch. 'You got no business here. I don't want you here and neither does Harker.'

The words stung, though she reckoned they should not have. They had never wanted her. That had not changed and never would. 'That why you moved around so much? Changed your name?'

A look of fear flashed across the older woman's face, one she tried quickly to hide. 'That's none of your business, way I see it.'

Tootie nodded, frowned. 'Maybe it isn't. But my brother *is* my business. I expect you know I came for him, not for you.'

'He ain't here.' Did the older woman shudder? Tootie wasn't sure, but something affected the woman with the mention of Alejandro.

'Where is he?' The words came hard, controlled and she braced herself for the worst.

*Please don't let him be . . . dead . . .*

Agnes Pendelton turned away, stared out through the window across the room. 'How the devil would I know? Ain't got no more interest in seeing him than I do you.'

37

Agnes's voice had hitched ever so slightly. Was there something she wasn't saying? Was the old woman hiding something?

'What happened to him after . . . you sent me away?'

The older woman shook then, a shudder that threatened to separate her thin flesh from her bones. 'He . . . he took your leaving hard. Wouldn't pay me or Harker no nevermind. Wouldn't do no chores, ignored his schoolwork. He became just another mouth to feed. He finally ran away about a year later. Never saw him again.'

In a way the news came as a relief, yet in another it filled her with hopelessness. If he had run off all those years ago the chances of finding him now were slim.

'You just let him run off alone? A ten-year-old boy? You never tried to find him?' Tootie's voice quivered with a mixture of anger and pain.

The older woman laughed without humor. 'Why would we? Told you we didn't want kids. Your parents practically forced you on us. What could we say when they asked us to take you in if anything happened to them? No? Wasn't a choice, but when they were gone ... well, nothing to say you couldn't go to that home or he couldn't go off on his own. He was a clever boy. I reckon he made well for himself.'

Crimson flooded Tootie's face. 'You're a monster, Agnes. You made a promise to my parents their children would be provided for, given a home, a chance to overcome what fate had done to them. Those children needed you and Harker and you abandoned them.'

The older woman let out a jeering laugh. 'You been waiting all these years to tell me that? Well, you've had your piece, now feel free to ride away and never come back. I ain't lookin' for any forgiveness from you or him. And if you think I give a damn about you now, you best think again. Like I said, we don't want you here. *Ever*.'

Tootie nodded, despite her anger at

what they had done to her brother, feeling almost deadened to her aunt's cold words. 'Strangely enough, Agnes, I forgave you a long time ago. I reckon whatever accounting you got coming will be between you and your Maker when your time comes.'

'Reckon that's my cross to abide.'

Again Tootie saw some sort of fear whisk across the older woman's eyes but couldn't have cared less about the reason for it. She sighed, struggling with her composure.

'You certain you have no idea where he might have gone?'

'No ... none a'tall. That all you came for?'

Tootie frowned. 'Reckon I couldn't expect anything more.' She turned to leave, grasping the door handle, pausing, then stepping out onto the porch. She left the door open behind her.

After untethering the reins, she mounted her horse, then looked back to see her aunt standing at the door, gripping the wood, edge pressed to her cheek. An odd expression rode Agnes Pendelton's eyes, unfathomable, but it didn't matter. Hope was lost and her brother was likely just another victim of the west. Ten-year-old boys seldom survived on their own.

A tear drifted down her cheek as she swung the horse around. Another glance back and she saw the door was shut, closing the opening to her past, likely forever.

And it hurt like hell.

She kicked the horse into a gallop, hands clutching hard to the reins as she whipped across the yard. The woods opened at the edge of the property and she sent the mount onto the trail, riding with little sense of her surroundings or welfare until about a mile down when she saw a man on horseback awaiting her. She rode up to him, angling to the side, letting him see the pain in her eyes, the tears on her face. It was an act of trust she had thought she would never indulge in, allowing another see her weakness, glimpse her soul. But for all he had done for her, Jim Hannigan deserved that trust, that vulnerability. She only hoped he would return it someday.

'You spoke with her?' His voice came low, soothing. His hazel eyes held warmth, comfort, and his rangy frame was relaxed, open to her. She had asked him to remain here, let her do what she needed to do alone. He hadn't cared for the idea a lick, but had understood and relented.

She fought to steady her voice, and another tear slipped from her eye, tracing a path down her cheek. 'She told me she never wanted to see me again, neither of them did. She told me they never wanted me or my brother.'

He drew a breath, nodding, face grim. 'About what you expected . . . '

'Reckon.'

He frowned. 'But hurts like a sonofabitch all the same.'

She nodded, lips quivering, emotion burning in her throat. 'Your brother?' he asked.

'She told me he ran away a year after I was sent to the home. She didn't know what happened to him beyond that.'

He looked ahead, as if uncomfortable with her raw emotion, uncertain how to handle it. He wasn't a man used to dealing with feelings, she knew that. He was trying, but it came hard.

'We'll keep looking, Tootie. I promise you. Every resource I got I'll use to find him for you.'

She shook her head. 'There's no place to start. Trail's cold.'

'Maybe, but that won't stop me from trying just the same.'

He meant it and she was thankful for it, for him, but still her despondency strengthened. She'd felt alone before, that was nothing new. But the knowledge that her brother had run off made it feel as if a part of her had died today. As if fate had rescued her from that river only to drown her in hopelessness so many years later.

'We have a job to do . . . ' she said.

43

'We best get to it.'

A grim expression cinched his lips, and she knew he didn't know what else to say. She gigged her horse into a trot and a moment later he followed suit.

* * *

Rajas Vago sat his horse on a bluff a few hundred yards from the Pendelton homestead. Darkness crept across his face, and his lips drew tight, his one eye narrowed. Avara Ganado reined up beside him, gazing down at the modest cabin, puzzlement on his features.

'*This* is the place?' Ganado shook his head. 'Don't look like it's worth risking our necks for. Just some rancher's spread, not even a prosperous one. Can't be nothing there of value.'

Both men wore inconspicuous clothing, denim shirts and battered Stetsons, brown trousers. If seen, they would have been mistaken for just another pair of cowboys, with no association to the traveling carnival. Ganado had

44

replaced his jeweled knives with a Smith & Wesson for the time being.

Vago uttered a small sound of disgust. 'Oh, but there *is* something of great value there, something I've waited a lifetime to find.'

'What?' Ganado's eyes narrowed, as he peered at Vago. 'Can't be any money in a rundown dump like that.'

Vago cast Ganado a patronizing look. 'You wouldn't understand, Ganado. Has nothing to do with money . . . unless you consider it a debt paid in full.'

'You know who owns the place?' Ganado's gaze went back to the rundown building.

Vago stifled a small smile of satisfaction. Ganado might have started to doubt his employer's good sense, as well as his sanity, but Vago knew damn well what he was doing. He'd waited years for this day. How many nights had he spent trapped in nightmares of the day those who owned that house had torn from him the only thing he gave a damn about? His heart began to drum with the anticipation of putting an end to those nightmares — and to the soulless bastards who had made him the man he was today.

'I know . . . '

Ganado's horse snorted. 'We goin' down?'

Vago nodded, the smile coming to his lips now. 'Reckon we are.'

Ganado's head lifted and he tensed. 'Wait — somebody's comin' out of the place.'

Vago's face went white. For an instant a tremor shuddered through him. Unable to find his voice, he merely stared at the young woman who came from the home and mounted the horse tethered to the rail. He watched the door close, then the young woman ride hell-bent for the trail at the opposite end of the property.

'I'll get her.' Ganado gripped his reins tighter. 'I reckon whatever you got in mind isn't something we need a witness for.'

46

Vago found his voice then, as a surge of anger sizzled through his veins. 'No! Leave her be.'

'Are you plumb loco?' Ganado gave his partner a shocked look. 'We had enough trouble in that last town, we don't need — '

Vago had his gun drawn and aimed at Ganado's face in a heartbeat. His finger bleached on the handle and death rode his gaze. 'I said leave her be.'

Ganado didn't move, fury and fear playing in his eyes. 'Put that away, Vago. I ain't your whipping boy.'

Vago's gaze locked with Ganado's. After a dragging moment, his better judgment took over and he holstered his gun. 'You been questioning my orders too goddamn often as of late. I don't like it.'

Ganado's face had gone crimson. 'You been taking too many damn chances. I've got no hankering to get my neck stretched.'

'You worry too much — yah!' Vago heeled his horse into a downward plunge, heading for the house. He felt giddy with bloodlust, the fever of vengeance flooding his veins. 'Welcome home the prodigal son . . . ' he whispered. 'Been a long time wanderin'.'

When he reached the homestead, he jumped from the saddle, pausing before the steps to the porch. Ganado reined up, only a few paces behind him, dismounted.

Vago peered at the closed door, tongue pressed to the back of his top teeth. He drew his Smith & Wesson a second time, palm damp, heart a jackrabbit. Taking the stairs without sound, he went to the door and rapped on it, a flood of memories struggling to free themselves and overwhelm his mind.

The door opened suddenly. 'I told you we don't want you here — ' The old woman's shout stopped dead the moment her gaze locked on the man who stood on her doorstep. 'Jesus Lord . . . ' she muttered, voice faltering.

'Not even close,' Vago said.

She tried to slam the door in his face but he jammed the heel of his left hand against the panel and shoved. The door careened inward, along with the old woman. She stumbled backward, lost her balance and landed on the floor on her rear, dazed.

Vago entered the house, Ganado following and closing the door behind them.

'You expecting someone else, Agnes?' Vago peered about the small room, which looked plain as a cheap whore's shack. 'Maybe you thought that woman who just rode off had returned? No doubt she was quite a bit kinder than I intend on bein'.'

The old woman looked at him with fear in her eyes, no, not fear: terror, pure and white hot, as if the Devil had come a-callin'.

Vago reckoned that was damn close to right.

'What do you want here? Get out. Get out of my house.' Her voice

49

trembled but he had to give the old bitch credit for backbone.

Vago laughed, a sound that made the older woman shudder. 'You moved around a lot, Agnes, a whole hell of a lot. Changed your name a few times, too. You afraid of something, Agnes? Afraid old debts would come due?'

'P-please . . . we're old, let us be . . . ' Her words came barely audible. She gripped the edge of the sofa, pulled herself onto it.

Vago stepped deeper into the room. 'Let you be? After spending so many years hunting you and Harker down? You and I both know that ain't in the cards, don't we, Agnes? You and I both know you got to pay for what you done.'

'I didn't do anything!' Her voice grew shrill, trembling.

'Reckon that's the most honest thing you've said in quite a spell, ain't it?'

Ganado's head turned, as if he heard something outside, then he looked back to Vago. 'She's just an old woman, Vago, maybe we should just go before — '

Vago didn't bother to glance back at his companion. 'Don't let her looks fool you, Ganado. She's meaner than Old Nick himself. She knew this day would come. She knew I'd never stop looking for her.'

Ganado's features tightened. 'Someone's coming, Vago. I heard a horse. That girl might've — '

'No, she wouldn't come back. I saw the look on her face. Just another sin this old hag has to atone for.' He turned and waited, staring at the door. A moment later heavy bootfalls clomped up the steps and across the porch. The door rattled open, and Ganado stepped aside, gun now drawn.

Vago swung his own aim to the man who entered and stopped short upon seeing them.

'What the hell — ' the man started, then his mouth clamped shut. His face reflected the look of a man who'd spent too many years on the run. His hands carried a permanent tremble and his clothes were worn beyond good use.

Vago smiled. 'Welcome home, Harker. Been a spell, hasn't it?'

'You . . . ' Harker appeared riveted where he stood, spite glinting in his sundown eyes.

Vago's smile widened, the grin of a snake about to swallow a mouse. 'Glad to see you haven't forgotten me. Most folks wouldn't recognize me with the patch an' all.'

'Ain't likely to ever forget that look you got in your eye.' Harker shook his head. 'Same one as the day I last saw you. Time ain't changed you.'

'Oh, but it has. Might be the one thing I can thank you for. The years made me stronger, capable of things I never would have imagined had events gone different. You know it, too, else you wouldn't kept on the run all these years.'

'What do you want?' Harker said.

'Want? Why, that hasn't changed, either. Told you the day I left what would happen when I came back.' A blast filled the room, deafening, shocking. Ganado nearly fired by reflex as he came half out of his skin.

Harker Pendelton jolted, a round hole appearing in his chest, a crimson aura about it widening rapidly. Then he pitched backward and with a thunderous bang hit the floor flat on his back.

'Jesus, Vago!' Ganado said, face washing pale, despite the fact he'd seen Vago kill numerous times before.

The old woman began shrieking and Vago swung towards her. Tears streamed from her eyes as she stared at the body of her murdered husband. Vago smiled. Who would have thought Agnes Pendelton could have given a damn about anyone other than herself?

The shrill wailing rode his nerves and he leveled the gun on her. 'It could have been different, Agnes. Different choices, different lives.'

'You bastard!' she screamed, trying to leap off the couch and at him, all sense of self-preservation gone.

He didn't give her the chance. He fired once and the bullet punched into her forehead, kicking her back onto the couch in a lifeless heap.

He stared at what he'd done, thinking he should have felt somehow more appeased than he did. It was just over, strangely anticlimactic, after dreaming of this day for such a long time. Over and yet, he still had one piece of unfinished business, didn't he? The young woman who had left here earlier. That brought a certain measure of contentment to him, one he'd thought he'd never experience again.

'Vago, we best ride before someone else comes.' Ganado motioned to him and Vago nodded, slipping his gun into its holster.

As Rajas Vago left the house, closing the door on the bodies within the room, he reckoned he was also closing the door on one part of his past, while stepping forward into another. He glanced at the trail the young woman had taken, a wafer smile coming to his lips.

'Tooties don't float . . . ' he whispered, then went to his horse.

# 3

Payton Thompson hunched over a small table in the rundown hotel room, a death grip on a whiskey bottle and an amber haze shimmering across his vision. He glanced about the sparsely furnished room, which held a lumpy bed with dingy sheets, a half-dresser with a porcelain basin and pitcher, and the chair upon which he sat. He belched, then scratched his chest, his undershirt soaked with dribble, stained with the remnants of his breakfast.

Where the hell *was* that gypsy, anyway? Shouldn't she have been here by now? It was what, near to eight? He drew his timepiece from a pocket, struggled to focus on the hands. Half-past seven. Damn, she wasn't due for another half-hour. Felt like she was late, though, but he'd started drinkin' early today, and a half-dozen shots of redeye did funny things to a man's sense of time.

He hoisted the bottle and jammed it to his lips, swallowing a deep drink, enjoying the sensation of the rotgut burning its way to his belly. Hell, it tasted like cat piss, but most of his money was earmarked for that gypsy he'd encountered earlier at the circus visiting Angel Pass, so he couldn't be too particular about his libations. That the gypsy sold more than fortunes had come as a pleasant revelation, one he was anticipating with great eagerness since that no-good bitch of his had packed up her bags two weeks ago and deserted him, while he'd been away at the saloon, gambling. She wasn't half bad lookin' for a chili-eater, either, better'n most of the whores in this town.

'Hope she likes things rough,' he mumbled, because he was of a mind to take out some of his pent-up fury with his woman on all their kind. Wouldn't be the first time he'd beaten the hell out of a whore.

A tap sounded on the door and his head jerked up. Hell, she was early.

Letting go of the bottle then gripping the table edge with both hands, he hoisted himself to his feet and waited a ten count for the room to stop spinning. A bolt of nausea surged into his gut, but he forced it down. Wouldn't do to puke all over the entertainment, would it?

He stumbled to the door, fumbling with the handle until he managed to turn it enough to pull the door open.

The young woman who stood in the hall looked like heaven to a sinner, but she wasn't the same gypsy he had met earlier that day. She was dressed like a gypsy, certainly, in an off-the-shoulder blouse and a skirt that hugged her slim hips. An array of silver and gold bracelets encircled her right wrist and her blue-black hair was done in tight curls, partially covered by a flowered, blue kerchief. Large loop earrings framed either side of her Mex-spiced face. Her modest bosom disappointed him, but what the hell, she was a damn sight better looking than the other gal.

'Who ... the hell are you?' he managed to get out, mostly a gurgle.

The woman smiled. 'Why, Madam Mystique discovered she had another obligation and couldn't make it, so she sent me instead. My name's Tootie. That get your sap runnin'?'

A stupid grin spread across his lips. 'Shore as hell does!' He let out a liquidy laugh, spittle gathering at the corners of his mouth. 'You an' me, we're gonna have a right fine time.'

Her smile widened, and a self-satisfied glint played in her eyes, which he might have wondered about had his head not been swimming with redeye and lust.

'Just one little thing ... ' Her expression turned coy and she dragged an index finger down his chest, then giggled.

'Yeah, what's that?' He hoped she wasn't going to demand more money for being better looking, because he figured he deserved a discount for the lack of tit.

'You wouldn't mind if my friend joins us, would you?' She batted her eyelashes.

'Friend?' he mumbled, eyes narrowing.

A *skritch* sounded from beside the door, and he glanced over to see the muzzle of a sawed-off Peacemaker inches from his face. A man stepped from around the corner of the door and Payton backed into the room.

'What the hell — ' He thought about going for his gun but realized he'd left his gunbelt hanging over the back of the chair and would never make it over to it on his unstable pins before the man blew his brains out.

'Name's Jim Hannigan. Got a dodger on you for killin' a woman over in Stagger Bend. I'm takin' you in for murder.' The bounty man's rangy frame remained relaxed, ready for the slightest resistance or threat on Payton's part. The girl laughed and it annoyed the hell out of his rapidly sobering mind.

'That wasn't no woman, that was a no-good whore who stole — ' He clamped his mouth shut, realizing he wasn't quite sober yet and had just blurted out a confession of sorts to a mankiller.

Hannigan's expression remained serious. 'Reckon you can come peaceably or in a box, choice is yours and which way don't matter a lick to me.'

Payton eyed him, then the girl, and decided a chance at a trial later was better than a bullet here and now. 'I'll go . . . '

Hannigan glanced at Tootie. 'You got the paper on the gypsy?'

She nodded, patting her skirt pocket. 'I can handle her, don't worry.'

'I'll get him over to the marshal in Stagger Bend, then come back. Just keep her entertained for a short spell.'

Jim Hannigan motioned with his gun and Payton stumbled out into the hallway. 'We'll be goin' out the back way, just in case your gypsy friend decides to come early.'

Payton glared at him, but went in the direction Hannigan indicated.

★   ★   ★

When the manhunter and his prisoner reached the end of the hall, Tootie closed the door. Glancing about the room and seeing the whiskey bottle and seedy accommodations, she shook her head in disgust, then went to the edge of the bed and sat, waiting.

Five minutes later she knew Hannigan had been smart to leave the back way because a knock sounded on the door. Tootie smiled. Her quarry had arrived, the one with whom she planned to change places at the circus visiting Angel Pass and needed out of the way for a few days.

She pulled the arrest paper out of her skirt pocket and flipped it open on the bed. Seems Madam Mystique was sought for questioning in some light-fingered business involving a few other men she had seen fit to charge for services that little resembled gazing into a crystal ball. The law wouldn't be able to hold her for long based on the mostly circumstantial evidence, but Tootie hoped it would be long enough to get the job done.

She stood, reached into her pocket again and drew out a derringer, palming it as she headed for the door. Pulling the door open, she gazed upon the startled gypsy standing in the hall. The woman was dark-haired, full Mex blood and dressed nearly identically to Tootie, except for a much larger blouse size.

'Do come in, Madam Mystique.' Tootie showed her the business end of the derringer and motioned.

'I don't service women,' the gypsy said, mistaking Tootie's intent.

'Really? I heard rumors otherwise.' Tootie laughed and gestured with the derringer again.

The gypsy scowled, but stepped into the room.

Tootie was normally an expert at reading character, judging what a quarry might do, but the gypsy took her completely by surprise. The fortune-teller, as she entered the room, hurled herself sideways without even the slightest warning. The woman must have practiced the move countless times, likely to deal with men such as Thompson, who might be inclined to bang them around. The move knocked Tootie off balance and the derringer popped once; the bullet buried itself in a wall.

The gypsy wasted no time resting on her laurels. She snatched a jeweled short-bladed knife from her skirt and dove at Tootie before she was able to aim her derringer again.

Tootie barely managed to swing the little gun up to deflect the knife blade, which skidded against metal and missed her throat by fractions of an inch.

A blood-curdling screech that would have done a Comanche proud came from the gypsy, who did her damnedest a second time to skewer Tootie.

This time Tootie recovered her balance enough to bring up her free hand to catch the gypsy's wrist and give it a sharp twist. With a bleat of pain, the gypsy dropped the knife. In the effort to subdue the woman, Tootie lost her grip on the derringer, which hit the floor without discharging. The gypsy kicked it, sending it skidding across the room.

Tootie hated fighting women. With men, it was pretty straightforward: they swung, they missed, she took advantage of that, used leverage against them. With women of the gypsy's ilk it was a whole other kettle of fish. She found herself engulfed in a cyclonic flurry of biting, scratching, hair-pulling and jabbing elbows that would have done a bobcat proud.

An elbow thudded off her upper chest, forcing a burst of air from her lungs and for an instant making her vision stutter. She let out a grunt and shook her head to get it clear — just in time to see the gypsy's fist sailing towards her.

She wanted to scream 'Not the face!' considering she was going to try to finagle this woman's job in a day or two, but that wasn't an option. Snapping her head left, she took a glancing blow she hoped wouldn't leave a bruise.

The gypsy flailed and kicked, shrieked and spat, tried to sink her teeth into Tootie's arm.

'That'll be enough of that!' Tootie blurted, doubling a fist and burying it in the gypsy's bread-basket.

The gypsy folded and Tootie followed with two more blows to the woman's face that stunned her into a backward stagger.

Tootie rushed her, intending to finish the job but the gypsy recovered remarkably quick. She grabbed Tootie and they stumbled sideways over the small table. The table went with them and the whiskey bottle sailed through the air, splashing amber liquid across the floor and a wall.

Tootie landed hard on a shoulder, partially atop the gypsy woman.

The gypsy kicked and became a hurdy-gurdy of elbows and knuckles. Tootie tried to avoid the blows, at the same time endeavoring to keep her blouse from coming down. In the heat of the fight, the gypsy apparently didn't have the same sense of modesty, because her own blouse was suddenly bunched at her waist, revealing her more than ample attributes.

Tootie grabbed the woman's thudding fist and twisted; the gypsy let out a shriek of pain. Seizing the temporary lull in whirling limbs, she snapped a fist straight into the woman's temple, stunning her. She followed with three quick blows that made her knuckles ache. The woman lay still, breathing heavily, drooling out of one side of her mouth.

Climbing to her hands and knees, Tootie panted, hoping nothing major was broken or bleeding on her person. She yanked up the gypsy's blouse — no need of Hannigan coming back and getting a gander at *that*, she reckoned.

After getting to her feet, she recovered her derringer and tucked it into her skirt. She examined herself in a murky cracked mirror above the dresser and discovered herself no worse for wear other than a scratch or two, and let out a relieved sigh.

Plucking the woman's jeweled knife from the floor, she went to the bed, grabbed the sheet, and cut two strips of cloth from it. With these she bound the gypsy after heaving her into the chair.

She slapped the woman hard, if for no other reason than being too well endowed. She was surprised she was capable of such jealousy for no reason, but the slap sure as hell felt satisfying.

Going to the bed, she sat on the edge, wondering how bad Hannigan was going to tease her over having trouble with the supposedly easy capture of a lone woman. With the thought, she had half a notion to slap the gypsy again.

# 4

Angel Pass sprawled over a vast area, its broad main street rutted, inundated with puddles from the previous night's rain, and lined with false-fronted buildings. The street forked at its north end; side streets branched out in a webwork containing numerous shops and cafés, saloons and banks, hotels and boarding-houses, and various offices. Townsfolk bustled along the boardwalk, vanishing into stores, eateries, or rushing towards the carnival near the north junction.

Dressed in her gypsy outfit, Tootie del Pelado, strode along the boardwalk, aiming for that carnival. She figured she'd given them enough time to miss their fortune teller and be eager to hire a replacement. She doubted securing the job would be a cakewalk, however. If the troupe were guarding secrets, they would suspect a stranger and likely resist anyone getting a close look at their operation.

She smiled, confidence lifting her chin and straightening her carriage. She reckoned she could talk a man into just about anything and carnie fellas were just as red-blooded as cowboys. She had womanly weapons Hannigan could never match. She giggled. She wagered he was just relieved she wouldn't be displaying her wares as a bargirl again.

Stepping off the boardwalk into the street, she headed towards the traveling show that had erected their tents over a couple hundred yards of ground just fifty yards ahead. She spotted a number of wagons, most pancled, many ornate, with elaborate designs and vivid colors. Some wagons carried painted scenes, while others were adorned with wood carvings or fancy gilded mirrors. Wheels came in blue, red, and gold and sides were festooned with variegated plumes. A team of draught horses pulled each vehicle. The largest wagon boasted the legend: *Vago's Traveling Menagerie and Wondrous Oddities.*

Rajas Vago. A bit of an enigma, a man without much of a past to investigate, or at least one that was public. The man was either clean as a choirboy or a master at covering his indiscretions. She bet she knew which.

According to their research, Vago owned the show, ran it with his second-in-command, Avara Ganado. Ganado's past was equally vague, though they had dug up an arrest warrant for an altercation in a saloon that had amounted to nothing more than a couple days in the hoosegow. The most sinful of the lot, at least on paper, had been the gypsy, now sitting in a cell in Stagger Bend.

The circus traveled from town to town across Colorado Territory, a compact band of about fifty composed of jugglers, clowns, sword swallowers and dwarfs, ventriloquists and fire eaters, and a motley assortment of human oddities. Folks handed over their hard-earned wages to glimpse these pitiful folk, either out of some morbid curiosity or mean-spirited satisfaction at viewing another's misfortune. The thought of putting people on display made her stomach cinch, but she wasn't here to judge the show's moral character. She was here to stop something that portended to be far more appalling.

Townsfolk already crowded the pathways between the large tents and display wagons. Most of the tents sported signs that proclaimed various attractions, including Lady Python, Mistress of Reptiles; Karlito, the world's smallest man; Armir, the Persian Powerhouse, and show times for myriad acts. Her gaze settled on a wagon with the words Madam Mystique emblazoned on its side. It sat next to a plain wagon, around which milled juggling clowns, scuttling children and wandering customers munching roasted nuts and caramel apples. Overpowering scents of syrupy food and pungent horse dung filled the air, which felt crisp with autumn and rose goose-bumps on her bare shoulders.

Gaze roving again, she located the largest tent, deciding that was where Vago was most likely to be. With a sharp breath, she steeled herself and headed for the tent. Pulling back the flap, she entered, slipping into an act that promised she was far more than a mere gypsy, like their previous girl, who sold her favors on the side.

Gloom pervaded the interior of the tent. A desk of sorts — a large plank set across crates, two piled atop one another — sat near the rear. A heavy safe squatted a few feet from the desk and she glanced at it, wondering if it held records that might prove useful to their case, or if it merely protected the circus' earnings. She made a mental note to resolve that question as soon as she got the chance.

A number of folding wooden seats had been set up in the room; a man with dark hair and a look that said he wasn't any too happy to have someone wandering into the tent sat in one of them beside the desk.

'Mr Vago?' She coated her voice with as much honey and innocence as she could muster.

The man stood, shaking his head, and she noticed he had two jeweled daggers sheathed at either side of his waist.

'No, my name's Ganado. I'm Vago's second. You shouldn't be in this tent. The shows are all in the other ones.'

She took a few steps forward, casting him a sultry look she figured would have melted any man. 'I'm not here for the show, dumplin'. I'm a fortune teller, among *other* things. I'm looking for a job.'

Ganado's eyes narrowed, suspicion creeping into them. 'What makes you think we need one?'

'Oh, this town's not that large, sugar. Rumor has it your gypsy ran off with one of the town's more, how shall I say it, unseemly types. And on my way in I noticed her wagon was all closed up.'

Ganado studied her and she didn't care for the look in his eyes. She was having no effect on him, the way she did with most men, other than priests and fancies. She was willing to bet he was no priest, but he didn't look like the other type either.

'We don't need a fortune teller. She'll come back when she's had her fill of that fella.'

Tootie jutted out her bosom and clasped her hands behind her back, an angelic expression on her face. 'What if she doesn't? And even if she does, I could fill in for her in the meantime, maybe show you just how good I am at predicting the future.'

Ganado uttered a harsh laugh. 'You were any good at predictin' the future you'd know there's no chance in hell I'm going to give you a job here. We have a tight group. They don't welcome strangers.'

This was going to be a hell of a lot harder than she anticipated. She had expected a tough time persuading Vago, but she wasn't even piercing Ganado's armor and something in the man's eyes told her she never would. This man was nervous, protecting something, and not about to risk it by letting an unknown enter into the equation.

'If you'll just give me a chance, I could — '

'Get out.' Ganado's hand drifted to the hilt of one of his daggers, the meaning clear.

'Please, I really need the job and I could do, you know, other things . . . ' She put silk in her tone but saw no impression other than annoyance in Ganado's eyes.

'I won't ask you again nicely — '

'Hire her.' The voice came from a flap at the left rear side of the tent and both turned their heads in that direction. A man had entered, a man wearing a patch and a thick black beard. Her gaze narrowed, a strange feeling of familiarity taking her, then passing as she figured it must be because she knew this had to be Vago, the owner.

'What?' Anger jumped onto Ganado's face. 'You can't be serious!'

Vago's gaze locked on his second, brooking no argument. 'I said, hire her. We need a fortune teller and this woman has more looks than the last one. She'll bring in plenty. Every fella in town will want his fortune read.'

Ganado stared, open-mouthed, at Vago, clearly furious and more than a little shocked.

Vago stepped deeper into the tent, walking up to Tootie, taking her hand and kissing it lightly. 'I'm Rajas Vago. I own this show.'

'I'm — ' She almost slipped and gave her real name, catching herself at the last second. 'Hannah. Hannah Garret. But I reckon I'll go by the name Madam Mystique. I wouldn't want you to have to repaint the wagon.'

He laughed, a peculiar, humorless thing. 'No, we wouldn't want that, would we? There's a table and a crystal ball in the wagon you'll work out of. I'll have Karlito open it up for you for this evening's business.'

She put a coat of fake appreciation into her voice. 'Thank you for your kindness, Mr Vago. I won't disappoint you.'

His eyebrow arched above his good eye. 'No? I certainly hope not. I'm not a man who takes disappointment well. It's a weakness, I reckon. I can't abide with weakness.' Something lurked behind his words but at this point she wasn't certain what it could be. She only knew that both these men were up to something and the woman who'd hired Hannigan had been right to suspect their deeds.

She winked. 'I'll do the first night free, just to make sure you're satisfied.'

He studied her, his look unreadable. 'The other gypsy we had, she did ... *things* ... for extra money. We'll have none of that from you.'

'What?' snapped Ganado, incredulity in his tone. 'For Chris'sakes, Mystique earned a hell of a lot with those — '

'Avara!' Vago spun on his second, and Ganado backed up a step, went silent.

The circus owner turned back to Tootie, his face softening. 'Like I said, no whoring. That clear?'

She nodded, wondering why he had decided on that. Not that she would have been doing it anyway, but this way made the job a lot easier. 'It's clear.'

'You'll sleep on the floor in your wagon, way the rest of the crew do in theirs. Karlito will bring you a bedroll after the last marks are gone.'

'Marks?'

He smiled, an unpleasant expression. 'Marks. Customers, if you prefer.'

She nodded and began backing to the front of the tent. 'I'll see you later today, then.'

His smile widened and he didn't take his gaze from her.

She hesitated at the entrance. 'Have we . . . met before?'

He shrugged. 'I meet lots of folks in our travels. It's possible.'

His tone was odd, and she wondered if for some reason he was hiding the fact they had indeed crossed paths. He had hired her without question and that made her nervous. If he suspected who she was . . .

'Maybe you just have one of those faces . . . ' she mumbled.

He laughed. 'I'm sure that's it. The West is full of one-eyed bearded half-breeds.'

Under other circumstances she might have been embarrassed at her slip, but something about him sent a shiver of unease down her spine.

She couldn't put her finger on it, but something about Mr Rajas Vago told her nothing here was as it seemed and he had hired her for his own reasons. Reasons that maybe went deeper than a simple cat and mouse game with a possible agent of the law.

Reasons that might shake her to her very soul if she discovered them.

★ ★ ★

'Jesus, Vago!' Ganado went to the tent entrance and gazed out at the departing figure of the woman his boss had just hired. 'What the hell you think you're doing? She's a plant of some kind. Maybe that last town sent her.'

Vago ran a finger across his lower lip. 'You think so? A woman? How many women bounty hunters have you come across?'

'Well, none, but she might be working with someone else. You don't think it's goddamn strange Mystique ran off suddenly after working for us for over three years? No word, nothing? I checked the hotel where she was s'posed to meet that fella. She was seen going in but no one saw her come out. The fella, either.'

Vago nodded, a distant look glazing his eye as he stared straight ahead at the tent flap. 'Yes, I suppose it is odd. But better the devil you know than the one you don't. We can keep an eye on her this way, work around her.'

Ganado let out a disgusted grunt. 'We can't take any kids this time. We have to lay low, just be satisfied with the proceeds from the show for a spell.'

'We'll see.'

Ganado knew what that meant. There would be no lull in the operation. He doubted Vago could even control his addiction to taking those children. He was going to get them all hanged.

With another grunt of disgust, Ganado stalked from the tent. He wagered that girl wasn't working alone and he intended to keep an eye out for whoever her partner was. Vago could risk his neck, but Avara wasn't about to be measured for a coffin.

# 5

With late afternoon, Jim Hannigan reined up in front of the Angel Pass Marshal's Office. He'd scouted the town covertly since the night he'd dragged Payton Thompson and Madam Mystique off to cells in Stagger Bend. He'd seen no signs of untoward activity from the circus folk, but wagered they might lay low after their gypsy vanished mysteriously. The gypsy herself had proved uncooperative and downright vicious all the way to Stagger Bend after making a number of overtures towards Hannigan, which he ignored, peeling her rattle all the more. Tootie had insisted on accompanying them and seen fit to clock the gypsy after each of the woman's lewd passes. The thought of it brought a ghost of a smile to Hannigan's lips.

Dismounting, then tethering the

horse to the post, he figured it was time he introduced himself to the local law and operated more in the open, while Tootie played the angles. Working with a lawdog was always a dicey prospect. Some who held to the letter of the law — and he respected that — weren't always comfortable with a man of Hannigan's reputation operating in their town. He couldn't blame them but it made matters more difficult. A few understood some outlaws were caught only because a manhunter either bent or downright waylaid the rules at times. It came down to a choice of leaving a killer free to murder again or stopping the threat permanently. Hannigan long ago had learned to abide with the moral implications — or perhaps ignore them to the point where they only haunted his nightmares.

Whatever the case, he hoped this marshal understood his position and the stakes at risk if a man named Rajas Vago were allowed to move on.

He stepped onto the boardwalk, a

stitch of worry over Tootie pricking his thoughts. She would be working so close to the target, risking her life again and that was something he reckoned he could never get comfortable with. This time it might prove even more difficult because he'd promised her free reign, despite his misgivings over her safety, but that was something he had to learn to live with if he wanted her with him. Her mood had waxed from somber to melancholy since confronting her aunt and discovering her brother had vanished. She'd refused to talk about it since that day on the trail, but he'd seen tears in her eyes in vulnerable moments, when she thought he wasn't looking.

Emotions, especially women's emotions, were just so damned . . . well, he didn't know what they were, only that he felt awkward and unsure as hell every time he thought about trying to make her open up to him about it. He found himself apt to say something idiotic and just make things worse, so mostly he kept his trap shut. He reckoned that wasn't helping a lick either.

Sighing, he gripped the handle, opened the door, then stepped into the office. The room was small, with three cells to the back, a rack of guns on the right wall and a desk to his left. The marshal looked up from behind the desk as Hannigan closed the door and removed his Stetson.

'Help you?' the man asked. The marshal was perhaps a score of years older than Hannigan's twenty eight, hair receding, graying at the temples, and muttonchop sideburns. Slim of frame, but in a wiry way, he carried an air of quiet strength.

'Name's Jim Hannigan. Marshal Wentworth. Reckon it's time I introduced myself.'

The marshal stood, nodding. 'I've heard of you. Never thought I'd see you in my town, though.' The lawdog's tone held neither approval nor condemnation and Hannigan reckoned that was a good sign.

Hannigan approached the desk, proffering a hand. The lawdog accepted it, his grip solid, unintimidated.

'Rode in from Tarrowville. A woman there hired me.'

'Woman?'

'Her husband was killed a short time back. They found his body along with four others on a trail leading from town. The men rode out hell-bent after something, but never bothered telling anyone their plans. Reckon they were a lynch party, though.'

'I hear tell you normally hire out for vengeance, not justice. That true in this case?'

'I reckon that's about what this woman wanted, but after I spent some time asking around I got another reason, and a few more folks who asked for my services.'

The marshal nodded, motioning to a chair in front of the desk. He lowered himself into his own seat as Hannigan tossed his hat on the desk and sat. 'S'pose you tell me the particulars.'

'This woman wanted her husband's killers brought down. While they hadn't told anybody their plans she had overheard him talking to one of the other men. What the townsfolk told me and some investigation on my own turned that into a working theory.'

'Care to elaborate on it?'

'Town lost some cash and precious stones, not a lot, but enough to raise a few eyebrows. But that's not what put these men in a posse mind. Seems a child disappeared, vanished as if he'd just stepped off the face of the earth.'

'Indians?'

Hannigan shook his head. 'Circus.'

The marshal's eyes narrowed. 'You don't mean the one parked at the north end of town, do you?'

'One and the same. I did plenty of checking. Appears nearly every town they have visited came up with missing children, jewels or gold. They move on before anyone figures it out usually, but this time some men got a notion the owner, Rajas Vago, was behind it.'

'And those men ended up dead?'

Hannigan nodded. 'All murdered and left on the trail leading out of town.'

The marshal's brow knitted. 'Surely if this Vago pulled this stunt in a number of towns somebody would have caught on and gone after him long before those men did.'

'Some fellas did go after them but there was a delay. When they caught up to the band and searched the wagons they found no trace of children or jewels. I figure Vago took advantage of the delay to dispose of his takin's.'

''Cept this time they didn't have enough time to do that and they murdered five men so they wouldn't be caught red-handed?'

'Way I figure it.'

'The show has been here two days. We've had no children come up missing or anything reported stolen.'

'How long they plan to be here?'

'From what I hear tell a week, give or take.'

'They likely wouldn't risk it until

they got ready to pull stakes. Give them a few more days.'

'So we just wait for them to take some kid?'

Hannigan nodded. 'Can't do anything legal about it till they make a move. I can't haul Vago to a county marshal on hearsay and no proof.'

'How you reckon on getting this proof? If they've been getting away with it this long, they're pretty slick customers.'

'Reckon they are, but I work with someone, someone who's trying to work her way inside as we speak. I aim to give her a little operating room, and take a look around myself shortly.'

A dubious expression crossed the lawdog's features. 'Won't a stranger put them on guard?'

'Likely. But nervous men make mistakes.'

'They may not make any move at all.'

'Always a risk, but I figure these sorts can't help themselves when it comes to stealing. They'll move. Angel Pass is too big a town for them to pass up.'

Marshal Wentworth shook his head. 'I dunno, Hannigan. Sounds like your plan hinges too much on circumstance.'

'You might be right, Marshal, but it's the best I got at the moment. I can't make any move until I get something solid on them, and that won't happen unless I get close enough to catch them in the act.'

'You really think these people take children? Why would they do that?'

Hannigan hesitated, swallowing hard at a knot of anger that cinched in his throat. 'Might be best not to ponder the reasons, Marshal. None of them are pretty.'

The marshal nodded. 'Need help, let me know. I got a deputy or two I can loan you.'

Hannigan stood. 'Much obliged. That's mostly why I stopped by, figured I'd let you know I was planning on lookin' into the troupe and to see if you had noticed anything out of the ordinary since they arrived.'

The marshal shrugged. 'Can't say they've been anything but noisy so far. I'll keep my eyes open, though.'

'Appreciate it.' Hannigan plucked his hat from the desk and set it on his head, then went to the door.

Once back out in the waning daylight, he felt a chill slither down his spine. He nursed his own doubts, the very same voiced by the marshal, and it made him worry about Tootie all the more. If Vago had no qualms about snatching children and murdering five men he damn sure would have none about killing a single woman.

The manhunter spent the next half-hour making arrangements at the livery for boarding his horse and transferring his saddlebags and Winchester to the room he had taken at a better hotel in town.

After settling the arrangements, he headed for the circus grounds, tipping a finger to his hat at women he passed, nodding to menfolk. No use looking anything other than the curious stranger for the time being.

As he walked onto the circus grounds he spotted a number of townsfolk at wagons and booths set up for refreshments. Some lined up at tents for early shows. Seeing clowns and jugglers milling about he suppressed a shudder. He'd always hated clowns. They usually showed up in nightmares with their hands gripping a gallows lever, face contorted in maniacal laughter. He saw nothing humorous about them, that was for damn sure.

Roughly fifty feet ahead he noticed a man casting him a surly look. The fellow was huge, well over six-feet in height, shirtless, despite the snap in the air, with brown skin and a heavy brow over piercing dark eyes. Black hair came nearly to the bottom of his ears. The man peered at him another moment then turned and vanished into a tent beside which sported a sign proclaiming: Armir, The Persian Powerhouse.

The sudden glint of metal hurtling towards him snapped his reverie. He caught the glint from the corner of his eye just as he rounded a plain paneled wagon next to the fortune teller's. Without an instinctive jerk of his head, the blade would have cleaved open a good portion of his scalp. It shrieked past his ear, thudding into the wagon.

His gaze jerked in the direction from which the knife had come. With a flash of clothing, a man vanished into the milling crowd.

Hannigan jumped forward, maneuvering his way through running children and wandering customers. The thrower was too far ahead, protected by the sea of people, for him to catch up to without an open path. He wound up jostling a few cowboys, who gave him threatening looks, but apparently thought better of impeding him when they saw the determined look on his face.

The chase led through an alley between two tents and around to the front of another. He glimpsed movement at a tent flap, and his hand whipped to the ivory grip of his stunted Peacemaker. As he eased up to the tent, he noticed at least two of the clowns had stopped to observe his actions. He drew his gun.

The wooden sign outside the tent boasted Lady Python, Mistress of Reptiles. Standing to the side and easing back the flap, he peered into the tent for any sign of his attacker. He hoped the thrower didn't carry anything other than the knife because the tent canvas damn sure would not stop a bullet.

Seeing no one, he entered, eyes and ears alert, Peacemaker roving. His nerves tingled and he suppressed an urge to shudder as his gaze fell on a makeshift pit roughly ten feet in diameter in the center of the room. Wire lined the sides, roughly three feet in height, with a small gate near the front to allow entrance. In the pit hissed at least fifty serpents of assorted types, slithering over one another. Christ, he hated snakes almost as much as he hated clowns. He backed up a step, no desire to get anywhere near the reptiles.

It took him only a moment to discern whoever had thrown the knife had gone out the back, if indeed he'd come in here in the first place. By now the trail was likely dead and Hannigan hadn't gotten a look at the man's features, so tracking him was dicey at best.

What concerned him was the promptness of the attack. It meant someone had recognized him, and that didn't happen often on looks alone. So far he'd only had contact with the marshal, livery man and hotel clerk, and he doubted any of them could have set up a trap so quick, even had they been suspect. None of them would have known he was coming here except possibly the marshal, but Hannigan's assessment of the lawdog pegged him as an honest man. Hannigan had staked him out for a day or so and researched his record before making the judgment call to take him into his confidence.

He slid the Peacemaker back into its holster and turned, stopping instantly as his gaze fell upon a woman standing in the tent entrance.

It was a rare occurrence when anyone was able to sneak up on him without him knowing it, but this woman had come up in utter silence, as if she were one of the serpents in her tent. That the tent belonged to her was obvious. A green body-fitting outfit showed every curve of her figure and far more flesh than Tootie would have appreciated him viewing. Snake tattoos encircled her arms and ankles. Her feet were bare and her hair, a reddish tangle, reached her shoulders. A black serpent coiled about her left wrist, its front end caressed in her opposite hand. Her eyes glittered like cold jade and the expression on her face was inviting, provocative.

'The show doesn't start for another hour,' she said, voice sultry, low-timbered. 'But you're a handsome fella. I reckon we could arrange a private performance.'

The offer pegged her as a whore as

well as a snake charmer, like the gypsy.

Hannigan, uncomfortable with the snakes and annoyed with himself over losing the knife-thrower, couldn't even force a smile. 'Reckon I'll let that opportunity pass. You see anyone come out of this tent?'

She smiled, but irritation played in her eyes. She wasn't used to being turned down. 'No one but you, gent. You a fancy? That why you don't want to take a tumble?'

Hannigan ignored the remark and angled around her to the flap. She shoved the snake towards him as he passed and he had all he could do to suppress a shudder. Her laugh followed him from the tent.

★  ★  ★

Rajas Vago looked up from his desk in the main tent as Avara Ganado came through the back entrance. Beads of sweat covered the second's forehead and his breath staggered.

'What happened?' Vago asked, leaning back in his chair, irritation prickling his nerves. Ganado was becoming a deficit, one he might soon have to cancel. 'You look like the Devil just pulled your marker.'

'A devil named Jim Hannigan.' Ganado's voice came with a gasp. He leaned against the table, panting.

Vago sighed. 'Who the hell is Jim Hannigan?'

'Christ, Vago, how could you not have heard of him? He's one of the worst of his kind.'

Vago arched the brow above his good eye. 'His kind being?'

'A mankiller. A fella who tracks down outlaws and more often than not brings them back in a box. Hear tell folks hire him when they're lookin' for vengeance. I reckon that's what got him on our trail. One of those folks who lost their kid musta called him in.'

Vago's gaze locked with his second's. 'So you threw a knife at him?'

Ganado's face went white, and shock

swept over his features. 'How the hell'd you know — '

'Don't look so surprised, Ganado. Works the same way our former fortune teller made her living, by noticing the little details. You left here wearing two knives at your waist. Only one there now.'

Ganado's hand instinctively went to the empty sheath at his hip. 'Oh, Christ, I left it in the side of the wagon.'

Vago laughed an annoyed laugh. 'Don't worry, one of our men's likely retrieved it by now if you were at all obvious about the attack, and I assume you were since it looks like you barely escaped with your tail between your legs.'

Ganado's face flushed from white to red. 'Look, you sonofabitch — '

Vago bolted up from his chair, grabbed his second by a handful of his shirt and yanked him close. 'I'm getting damn sick of your questions and screw-ups. You care to take that name-calling any further?'

Ganado went silent, then shook his head. Vago released him. 'I'm just saying if Hannigan's sniffing around here . . . '

'Who says he was sniffing? He might have been just passing through and stopped to take a look at the show. Course, now that you threw a knife at him he might be a little more interested in what's going on.'

'The hell! He's here for a reason. Someone over in Tarrowville set him on us. You still think it's a coincidence that girl showed up for a job and Mystique disappeared that way? They're working together, Hannigan and the new girl.'

Vago lowered himself back onto his seat, face tight. Ganado was right, it was too coincidental. But why would *she* work with a man like Hannigan?

'Have one of our men find out where he's staying. But for chrissakes don't be obvious about it.'

'What about the girl?'

'I'll keep a watch on her.'

The front flap of the tent flipped

back and a man came in, one who barely reached four feet in height, if that. Dressed much like an elf with green trousers, suspenders over a boiled white shirt, a pointed hat and black buckle shoes, his face was handsome, yet tainted with a look of sadness. He walked awkwardly up to Vago and dropped a jeweled dagger onto the desk.

'You should be more careful with your toys, Ganado,' the man said, glaring at the second, a patronizing expression coming onto his face. 'One of the clowns gave me this. Said he pulled it out of a wagon side after you threw it at a customer.'

'He wasn't a goddamned customer!' Ganado grabbed the blade and jammed it into the empty sheath. 'You best wipe that high and mighty look off your face before I do it for you, you little toad.'

The small man grinned. 'Eats at you knowing someone so small is your mental superior, doesn't it, Ganado?'

Ganado stiffened, a fist clenching.

'You goddamned deformed little — '

'*That* will be all, Karlito,' said Vago, stepping in before the two needed to be separated again. He had seen enough displays of their mutual hatred in the past to know one would likely kill the other one of these days. It was a wonder neither had already.

Ganado let out a disgusted grunt as the little man ambled from the tent, a thin laugh trailing him.

Vago glanced at Ganado. 'Get rid of those knives and find less distinctive ones. That bounty hunter might not have gotten a look at you but he damn sure saw that blade.'

Ganado nodded, then departed the back way.

Vago let out a heavy sigh, wondering if the Fates were starting to conspire against him.

★ ★ ★

Hannigan had spent a half-hour scouring the circus for his attacker, but as he expected came up empty. Whoever attacked him knew the layout of the grounds too well, knew where and how to hide, and Hannigan couldn't track sign with so many folks walking about, obliterating footprints.

When he went back for the knife, he discovered someone had beaten him to it, but that didn't surprise him, either. Dragging his fingers over the slice in the wood where the weapon had penetrated, he wondered if he should confront Vago, tell him he didn't appreciate being attacked, maybe throw a scare into him. Someone had recognized Jim Hannigan, so any element of surprise had gone up in smoke. After a moment of thought, he decided against a confrontation, at least until he contacted Tootie and found out whether she had infiltrated the show.

'Psst!'

The sound came from around the wagon. Hannigan's gaze shifted in that direction, every muscle tense. At first he saw no one. Starting around the wagon, he paused as the voice came again:

'Over here . . . '

Hannigan eased around the wagon, ready to go for his Peacemaker with the slightest provocation. His gaze settling on a man who barely came above his gunbelt, he stopped, relaxed his posture.

'Who are you?' Hannigan reckoned he'd never seen a person so small who wasn't a child. This one was dressed like pictures of elves he'd seen in a kid's book ages ago.

'My name's Karlito. I work for the circus.' The man's voice was light, airy, but his eyes held a note of sadness.

'As a what?'

'Mostly a target of insults and disgust.'

The sadness in the man's eyes deepened, and Hannigan could well imagine the way some folks might treat a fella so small. The West was a violent, unforgiving place, and anyone not up to some folks' standards made perfect targets for humiliation. Likely a job at a show such as the type Vago ran was the only option, but he reckoned even among oddities there was a pecking order.

'You know me?' Hannigan wondered just what the fellow was up to.

'In a way. Heard you being discussed. Figured you had to be the fella when I saw you looking for the knife.'

'Where'd it go?'

'One of the clowns found it, gave it to me. I had to give it back to its owner.'

'Who owns it?'

'Listen, gent, I can't be seen talking to you. They'd kill me if they found out. When we rode in I saw a saloon in town called the Golden Horseshoe. Meet me there tonight at 9, upstairs, room 2.'

'Why should I do that?' Hannigan folded his arms, studying the man for any sign of a trick, but something in Karlito's eyes said he was telling the truth. The man appeared weary, perhaps looking to unburden himself of some pent-up guilt.

'Because I can tell you what's going

on here and why it's happening. I'm tired of it, Mr Hannigan. I'm tired of feeling my insides churning every time we leave one of these towns with . . . well if you're all I heard, you can stop it. You can stop Vago and Ganado. I can't live with the guilt anymore.'

'What exactly *is* going on here?'

The little man's mouth clamped shut and he gazed about, worry on his features. 'I can't. If Ganado or Vago sees me talking to you . . . '

He scurried off, dashing under the plain wagon and out the other side. Hannigan let him go, not wishing to jeopardize Karlito's life if he were telling the truth. He'd meet the man at the saloon tonight, but he'd make sure if it were a setup whoever waited for him would have hell to pay.

★  ★  ★

A wry smile touched Jezebel Basco's lips as she leaned against the opposite side of the gypsy wagon, out of sight of

Jim Hannigan and that little turncoat, Karlito. The snake entwined about her wrist writhed, its tongue flicking, and she stroked its head. She uttered a silent laugh. She'd heard every word of their plan to meet later at the saloon.

So Hannigan thought he could simply reject her advances and walk away scot-free, did he? And Karlito, that stunted sonofabitch, she'd always been repulsed by him and his cringing every time he had to help her set up her snake tent. She'd imagined feeding him to one of her bigger snakes someday. Now she had her chance to get even with them both. Vago would be very interested in knowing what she had overheard. He'd likely pay her plenty in bonus for it, too. Ganado would be happy, too; maybe he'd even be rougher tonight when he bedded her.

She slipped from around the wagon and, after watching Hannigan walk away, headed for the main tent.

# 6

As dusk fell, Tootie returned to the circus, after informing Hannigan of her hiring by Vago. He'd told her of the knife attack and had expressed many of the same reservations about her role she felt herself.

He was right. Something was amiss. Vago had hired her on the spot and that was out of character for a man with something to hide, especially something as vile as Hannigan and she believed. Vago suspected her. And by now had likely tied her appearance at the circus together with Hannigan's arrival.

'He wants me close,' she whispered as she made her way towards the gypsy's wagon. That was the only explanation she could come up with. Vago knew she was more than whom she claimed to be, and he knew his gypsy hadn't vanished on a whim. So he was playing her close, keeping an eye on her. That meant she had to be craftier than usual, not allow any of the mistakes she had on recent cases.

In the meantime she needed to find a way to use Vago's suspicions and plan against him. He suspected her; she suspected him. Two could play the game and she'd spent far too much of her life since leaving the home being duplicitous, honing her skills, to let him come out on top. Vago was no different than any other man, no different than any other outlaw.

Well, he was different in one contemptible way. He kidnapped children.

Where had those children gone? She had kept her eyes open as she wandered the grounds earlier. None of the children she had seen belonged with the circus; all were with parents, coming to see the shows. She hadn't gotten any chance to search any of the wagons yet, but she doubted any of the kidnapped children, were they here and alive, would have kept quiet and not tried to escape.

That meant Vago had disposed of them somewhere and that gave her a shudder. She'd heard stories of men such as Vago, what they did with those they abducted. She said a silent prayer that such a fate wasn't the case here.

Reaching the gypsy wagon, she noticed the doors had been opened and swung back. Candles on a table towards the back lit the interior.

Hoisting her skirt, she took the wooden steps leading up into the wagon in two strides. The table also held a crystal ball and a wooden sign propped against a wall boasted the mysterious and all-seeing abilities of Madam Mystique. She reckoned it would be some trick faking a fortune teller's skills, but knew most of them worked from simple observation techniques, vague questions and evasive answers that lent themselves to a variety of interpretations applicable to about anybody.

'I trust you can work with this?' A voice came from behind her and she started, then turned to see Vago standing at the top of the stairs, peering at her. His one eye gave her the willies and the peculiar expression on his face didn't help matters. He was studying her, trying to see into her, and she'd let no man other than Jim Hannigan do that.

She was more than a little annoyed with herself for letting him sneak up on her, too.

*First night on the job and already a mistake . . . You won't live long if you keep that up, Tootie, my girl . . .*

'You came up on me damn quietlike.' She let some of the annoyance bleed into her voice. She reckoned a gypsy woman wouldn't back down to a fella like Vago. 'I don't like that.'

He offered a smile that missed the mark. In the flickering light from the candles and shadows of encroaching evening, his face looked more sinister than earlier.

'My humble apologies. Carnival folk are used to such things.'

'Are they?' She folded her arms across her chest, more to stop herself from shuddering than the look of defiance she was hoping to put across. 'Sneakin' around comes natural to carnie folk?'

'I don't have to sneak around. I own this troupe.' He stepped into the wagon. 'Probably best you understand that and leave such remarks unspoken.'

The threat behind his tone was obvious.

She nodded, then went to the table and settled into the chair behind it, hoping he wouldn't stay long. Something about him unnerved her more than she wanted to admit. The sense of recognition came again, and she struggled to place where she might have encountered him in the past but still couldn't figure it out. It was as if something got in the way, blocking the memory. That had never happened to her and she didn't care for it one bit.

'How'd you lose your eye?' she asked, hoping the question would take him off guard with its bluntness. 'Sneakin' around?'

He almost laughed, but instead turned to look out into the coming night. 'Happened when I was a child. Made the mistake of wandering into an outlaw camp. They thought it was great fun to taunt a child, someone considerably weaker than themselves. They took a burning stick and jabbed it at me, 'cept one of them misjudged. He was drunk.'

He went silent and she shivered at the thought of it, suddenly feeling sympathy for him.

'I'm . . . sorry. That must have been awful.'

He turned back to her. 'I can still smell the stench of my flesh burning. They let me go, but the damage was done. Half my world went dark.'

'The scar come from them, too?'

'No. Another time, another place. Cantina in Texas. Some men aren't fond of sharing their wives. But I was older and that man . . . well, I'm told it's inappropriate to speak ill of the dead.'

'You've had quite a life, I take it?'

'No, I've had quite an existence. Life made me as much a freak as some of the folk you see working here. That's why I run this circus. The deformed, the outcasts, I give them a place and together we are strong. We make folks come to us, pay us to gaze upon what they would otherwise mock.'

Bitterness laced his tone, deep and searing. He was a man of secrets, more than just whatever went on with this traveling show — the robberies, the abducted children. There was more, much more, a darkness she had little desire to peer into. With the revelation came a conflict of emotions within her, a simmering hatred for whatever this man was doing to innocent children, yet at the same time a strange sorrow and heartache for him at the way his life had led him to what he was now. It was something she rarely experienced for those she tracked, brought to justice.

'I'd best get started,' she said, voice low. 'Folks will be looking to have their futures foretold soon.'

He gave a slight bow. 'Yes, I suppose they will. The future. What will it bring . . . Hannah? What will tomorrow tell us? Next week? Will we recognize it when it's laid out before us?'

Her mahogany eyes narrowed. 'I'm not sure I get your meanin'.'

He smiled. 'No matter. All things will be revealed. That's what your sign says, does it not?' He laughed, picked up the wooden sign, then carried it down the stairs with him as he departed, leaving it propped against the wagon.

He was a strange one. The word freak might have applied perfectly, but another word came to her mind unbidden: evil. Rajas Vago was a devil in a town named after angels.

★ ★ ★

115

An hour later, after he made sure the final preparations for the shows were in order, Rajas Vago headed towards the main tent, startled suddenly when Avara Ganado angled up beside him. The Garret woman's questions had left Vago a bit more shaken than he had let on. Thoughts of the past always troubled him, memories of those years on the run, a child alone, fending for his very survival. That time had taken pieces of him, pieces of the man he might have become, and left them scattered across the dusty trails and blood-drenched nights of his youth.

He had told her he was as much a freak as those who worked the circus, but he had used the wrong word. Survivor, was the expression he should have used. They were survivors, all of them, survivors of some malevolent God Above's malicious joke. *He* was a survivor. He'd proven that by coming this far, by stamping out weakness wherever he found it, at the least his very own.

He would have thought all ties to his past died with Agnes and Harker Pendelton a few days ago. But he hadn't counted on *her* showing up. He'd believed her dead. He knew what usually became of girls on their own, sent away to homes. If they didn't wind up buried they ended up in saloons and cathouses selling their wares.

Was that what he had here? Another survivor? A woman who would do anything to prolong her existence? His conversation with her had revealed little but he wasn't about to come right out and confront her on the matter. At least not yet. Still, something about the way she questioned him made him think there was more to her than any whore or itinerant gypsy's lot.

Could she really be working with that bounty man, Hannigan? Had she somehow bucked the odds and turned herself into something lower than a whore, in his estimation, something little better than one of those do-good missionaries?

It sure as hell looked that way. He tended to side with Ganado's opinion on the matter, but like the sign said, all things would be revealed . . . and some things could be changed. She was a del Pelado, after all. A survivor.

'The little bastard's on his way,' Ganado said, snapping Vago from his thoughts.

Vago nodded, staring off at the sea of townsfolk milling about. 'He's weak. I should have figured he would have no stomach for what we're doing. You know what to do. Make sure he suffers . . . '

Vago walked away, leaving Ganado grinning with anticipation.

★　★　★

Jim Hannigan entered the Golden Horseshoe Saloon fifteen minutes before nine, alert for any sign of a trap. While he judged the dwarf to be telling the truth, he saw no use taking chances in his line of work. Arriving early would

118

give him an opportunity to scout the saloon and spot any hardcases or circus folk planted amongst the patrons.

The revelry was in full swing, cowboys from neighboring ranches pissing away their pay as fast as the watered whiskey and bad gin these places usually served. Durham smoke clouded the room and old sawdust littered the floor. The place reeked of cheap perfume, old booze and sweat.

Gathered around the dozen or so tables, men slapped down winning hands with whoops of joy or tossed bad-luck cards to the table while uttering curses. Dressed in peek-a-boo blouses or sateen bodices, whores with bored expressions leaned over their shoulders, waiting for the men to turn their attention from games of chance to games of bought passion.

A polished bar ran along the north wall, the barkeep behind it pouring whiskey into glasses on a tray held by one of the women. A gilded mirror hung behind the bar, glass dim, cracked. Paintings of nude women in alluring poses adorned the red-striped wallpaper.

He saw no one suspicious, neither outlaw nor circus type. In fact, everyone here appeared wholly engrossed in their games or women. That didn't mean they might not be feigning interest in the festivities, but he reckoned if the dwarf was setting him up, the trap would likely spring upstairs, away from the crowd, with any possible sounds covered by the clamor.

Hannigan took the three steps to the barroom proper and made his way for a staircase at the back of the room. He kept an eye open for any sign of someone watching him or making a move to follow him up the stairs.

As he reached the bottom of the stairs, a woman stepped from the crowd and grabbed his arm. One of the whores, her eyes carried the glazed look of a laudanum addict. He tried to pry her grip from his forearm and raise as little commotion as possible.

She giggled and held tight, her too-red lips moist with saliva. 'Hey, gent, take me for a tumble? I could be real nice to a handsome fella like yerself.'

'Some other time,' he said, breaking her hold and pushing her away. She glared at him, fists jamming to her thin hips and an indignant scowl creasing her lips.

'You couldn't do no goddamn better, gent, you know that?' Her voice waxed shrill and he worried she'd attract attention to him he little wanted. Last thing he needed was some drunken cowboy defending her honor and preventing the dwarf from showing up.

He smiled, dragging his fingers up her bare shoulder. 'Give me twenty minutes, then come up. I'll make it worth your while.' He reckoned he'd be far away from the saloon by then.

Her attitude flipped and she grinned. 'Now that's a damn sight better, gent. You won't be sorry. I'll be right special to yer.'

He nodded, then turned and headed up the stairs.

Foiled wall paper covered the hallway walls and a sconce held a kerosene lamp, flame turned low. It appeared deserted, but a tingle ran along his spine, that manhunter's sixth sense warning him something was amiss. His heart beat a step faster and he relaxed, ready to go for his Peacemaker at the first sign of threat.

Locating the second room, he eased over to it, and paused. The door had been left ajar, and that likely meant the dwarf was waiting on him already, but he wasn't going to take chances. His nerves buzzed now, blood rushing through his veins. Standing to the side and drawing his gun, shoulder to the jamb, he flattened his palm against the door panel, gave it a gentle shove.

The door creaked inward, then silence. That lack of sound ratcheted his sense of wrongness up another notch. Had Karlito been waiting in the room, the man would have made some sort of noise the moment the door swung in. That he hadn't meant he was keeping quiet on purpose — or had no choice. Neither prospect meant anything good.

Edging around the jamb, Hannigan froze. A single lantern on a nightstand lit the room, creating a macabre union of amber and shadow. The room held one occupant, but any trap that might have existed hadn't been set for Hannigan, it had been sprung on the little man from the circus.

'Christ . . . ' he muttered, stepping across the threshold and holstering his Peacemaker after a glance told him the room was empty of anyone living.

The dwarf's small body swayed from a rope suspended from the ceiling. His face was livid, tongue protruding, eyes bulging. Hannigan guessed he'd been dead for at least a half hour.

Going to the corpse, then unsheathing his boot knife, Hannigan sliced the rope above the dwarf's head, while enwrapping the body with his free arm. He lowered Karlito to the floor, then sheathed his knife and examined the dead man for any clue to whoever hanged him. In a pocket, partially sticking out, he discovered a slip of paper. Unfolding it, he saw one scrawled word: Leave.

A warning. Someone had seen the dwarf talking to him, had overheard the place and time and taken steps to make certain the meeting never took place. Whatever Karlito intended telling him had died with him.

A shriek startled Hannigan and he whirled to see the bardove he'd put off standing in the doorway, hands to her cheeks as she stared at the body of the little man. She kept shrieking and when he rose to his feet and started towards her she dashed from the doorway and scrambled down the stairs.

'Great . . . ' Hannigan whispered. He heard her shriek all the way down to the barroom and knew it wouldn't be long before he had company.

A few moments later the marshal stood in the doorway and Hannigan sat in a chair by the bed, waiting for him.

The lawdog had his gun out, and glanced at the body of the dwarf.

'One of the circus folk, I take it?'

Hannigan nodded. 'No need for the gun.'

'You kill him?' The marshal holstered his weapon.

'Ain't likely I'd be sitting here if I had.'

The marshal gave him a somber smile. 'What *are* you doing here?'

'This man . . . ' He ducked his chin at the body. ' . . . he told me he had some information about what was going on at the circus. His name's Karlito. Told me to meet him here at 9. I came up to find him hanging.'

'I've got a hysterical whore downstairs who says you did it.' The marshal went to the body, examined it briefly.

'Reckon she's seeing all sorts of things, from the look in her eyes.'

The marshal straightened. 'Figured her for a laudanum addict. Someone wanted to stop this fella from talking?'

'I expect. Pretty much solidifies my notion something's going on at the circus that doesn't involve sideshow attractions.'

'You know I'm going to need you in for questioning all the same? You were found in a room with the body.'

'Reckon that's what whoever killed him was hoping for. Thought he might take me out of the equation for a spell. I reckon you know damn well I had nothing to do with this man's death.'

The marshal let out a humorless laugh. 'Didn't figure a famous bounty man would ride in and start killing dwarfs after informing me of his mission, but Angel Pass is a peaceable town, normally. We have procedures for this sort of thing. You got your duty, I got mine.'

'I understand. Just don't take your time with it. I got a girl inside that circus. I don't want her on her own for too long.'

'I'll make it as painless as possible. Show up at my office in the morning and I'll take your statement. You're released on your own recognizance for the night. I expect you won't be leavin' town?' The marshal grinned and Hannigan returned the smile.

'Already got my bags unpacked and my horse boarded for the week.'

'Sorrowful thing.' The marshal shook his head, then nudged his chin towards the body. 'Little fella dressed like an elf gettin' strung up that way. Be silly under less grim circumstances.'

Hannigan's face darkened. 'Sometimes when folks try to do the right thing others don't take kindly to it. I'll see to it whoever did this pays for it.'

'Reckon it don't matter a lick to me whether the killer comes to me on two feet or in a box. Just find him.'

With a glance at the body, Hannigan felt sorrow rise for a man he had never known, and anger at whoever had preyed on someone who likely had little chance defending himself against a larger assailant.

He left the room, then went out a

window and down an outside stairway, wanting to avoid any chance of being detained in the saloon by the hysterical whore or anyone else looking to pin a murder on him. He saw nothing more he could do tonight, so he headed back to his hotel. Tootie had told him Vago expected her to sleep in her wagon and the thought made him antsy in light of tonight's events, but if he showed up at the circus to check on her he risked jeopardizing not only her cover, such as it was, but her life. While he felt certain Vago was only keeping her close for his own protection, he knew if anyone could use that against him, Tootie could.

He just hoped she didn't make a mistake and get herself hanged like the dwarf.

# 7

Jim Hannigan walked along the board-walk towards the marshal's office, holding to his promise of the night before, though he knew it would do little good. He had nothing to add to his story of finding the dwarf hanging from the rafters.

The sun chased some of the chill from the morning air. Brassy rays glinted from water troughs coated with thin skins of ice and glittered from windows. Patches of frost coating hitch-rails and ground depressions melted. A handful of folks sauntered along the boardwalk, heading for early-opening shops or the café. He'd killed a half-hour at the café himself with a quick breakfast of beef-steak and biscuits, but barely touched it. A pot of Arbuckle's helped wash some of the lethargy from his body, since he'd slept little the previous night worrying about Tootie at the circus. Sometimes he wondered just how the hell he was going to survive having her around. The only thing worse would be having her gone. A fella just couldn't win.

The marshal already sat behind his desk by the time Hannigan entered the office. The lawdog looked bleary-eyed and was nursing a tin cup of coffee.

'Offer you a cup? Tastes like manure but it'll keep you awake.'

Hannigan shook his head, pulling around the chair in front of the marshal's desk and straddling it, forearms resting on its back. 'Stopped by the café on the way over. Any more coffee and my teeth will be floating.'

The marshal leaned back in his chair. 'I moseyed on over to the circus late last night and had a parley with Vago. Told him his dwarf wasn't coming back and he needed to make arrangements for the body.'

Hannigan raised an eyebrow. 'Bet he wasn't too broken up over it.'

'Put on a show of it. Demanded your arrest for the murder after I told him you discovered the corpse.'

Hannigan nodded. 'Follows. He probably saw the opportunity as two birds with one stone. Set me up and get me out of his hair while disposing of a problem with his own worker. Confirms if I ever needed it someone there recognized me.'

The marshal's eyebrow lifted. 'You suspected that?'

'Someone tried to take my head off with a knife while I was there yesterday. Jeweled dagger, the kind knife-throwers use.'

'You got this knife?'

'Was gone when I went back for it, but the dwarf was waiting for me. He said it went back to Vago.'

'Makes the fella look damned suspicious, then, don't it?'

'Reckon more so by the minute.'

The marshal sighed, ran a finger over his lip. 'His second, a man named Avara Ganado, had two knives strapped to his waist. Figured him for the knife-thrower of the troupe, but neither was jeweled.'

'Likely he would have exchanged them for something less conspicuous after missing me and knowing sooner or later I'd go back to take up the incident with Vago.'

'Still, nothing I can go put his ass in a cell for.'

Hannigan folded his arms. 'Wouldn't do any good if you did. Figure that's why I need to get in, find something on them that leaves no doubt as to their guilt — even if I don't confine myself to the letter of the law doing it.'

The marshal laughed. 'Lots of lawdogs would be put off by a remark like that. But I got a notion the law don't always cover it when it comes to some outlaws. Till it does men like you will be a necessary evil, I reckon.'

'I'll take that as a compliment.' Hannigan grinned, but the whole thing annoyed him. He was used to controlling things more, working his way in and isolating the outlaw, then taking him out. Vago had already made a move against him, and in another town it just might have worked. He was lucky the marshal wasn't pressing matters.

'You know Vago might not give up trying to pin Karlito's murder on you?'

Hannigan nodded. 'He's not intimidated the way most outlaws would be, that's for damn sure. But I reckon he'll look for other tactics when that one doesn't work.'

'Which means he's either packin' two sets of balls or plain loco.'

'Only a loco man'd take children, I figure.'

The door rattled open and the marshal's gaze jumped to the woman entering. Hannigan's head twisted and he saw a young woman whose face was a mask of worry. Dressed in a simple skirt and apron, hair disheveled, she came into the room in a rush, blue eyes glimmering with tears.

The marshal came out of his chair and moved around to the front of his desk. 'Betsy, what's wrong?'

The woman came up to him, face pleading. 'Find him, Marshal Wentworth, find Caleb.'

'Caleb? He's gone? What happened?' The marshal's voice dropped and Hannigan's belly plunged with it. He stood, waiting for the woman to speak.

She had a difficult time composing herself and the marshal gripped both her arms firmly.

'Tell me what happened, Betsy.'

'He's a good boy, Marshal. He's never done nothin' like this before.'

'Nothin' like what, ma'am?' asked Hannigan.

The woman looked at him, as if afraid suddenly to reveal anything to a stranger.

'It's all right, Betsy. This is Mr Hannigan. He's . . . helping me on a case. You can say it in front of him.'

The woman shuddered as she looked back to the marshal. 'He ran away, Marshal. When I went in to wake him this morning for chores he wasn't in his bed. He was there last night when I read to him.'

'Now, calm yourself, Betsy. He's a nine-year-old boy and they're wont to wander off to the fishing hole before school. I'm sure by the time you get back home he'll be sitting at the table waitin' on his breakfast and lookin' innocent as all hell.'

'No, Marshal. Caleb wouldn't go off without tellin' me, not since Josh died. He thinks he's the man of the house now. He wouldn't run off fishing without tellin' me, but . . . '

'But what?' The marshal's voice held firm, comforting, and his gaze locked with hers.

'Well, he kept talkin' about that silly circus that's in town. He wanted to go the last two days but I kept tellin' him we didn't have any extra money. I hated denyin' him, he works so hard for a child. He does a man's work, you know.'

'I know, Betsy. It's been hard on you both since Josh died.' The marshal's voice had changed tone and he glanced at Hannigan, who gave a slight nod.

135

Hannigan had thought the same thing as the lawdog the moment the circus had come up.

'You think Caleb might have snuck off to see the carnival, ma'am?' Hannigan asked.

She stuttered a nod. 'I'm sure of it. He wanted to go so bad, just to see the clowns, even if we didn't have the money. I told him maybe near the end of the week, but he was stuck on the notion. He begged me every chance he got. I tucked him in last night and this morning he's nowhere to be found. Please, Marshal, go look for him.'

The marshal nodded. 'I will, Betsy. You go on home and I'll go right out there and take a look around. I'll check all the fishing holes, too, just in case.' He gave her a reassuring smile and she nodded, a tear streaking down her face. Backing away, she went to the door and let herself out.

Hannigan peered at the marshal. 'I got a sick feeling in my belly.'

The marshal's face went grim. 'So do

I. Reckon you'll be wantin' to come with me.'

'Does the Devil have horns?'

'This one sure as hell might.'

The marshal led the way from the office. Hannigan found himself cursing the flagrant move of the circus owner. Knowing he was being watched, investigated, Vago had thrown down the gauntlet, issued a challenge to Hannigan by snatching another child right under their noses. The man was either the world's most confident fool or just plain crazy.

The circus appeared mostly deserted when they arrived. Wagons had been shut down for the night and Hannigan's gaze jumped to the fortune teller's cart, the doors to which were closed.

'Reckon this Vago's an early riser?' the marshal asked.

'Don't much give a damn if he ain't, but if he is he'll likely be in the main tent, which I'm guessing is the big one over yonder.' Hannigan ducked his chin at the largest dwelling. The marshal nodded and they aimed for it.

Two men occupied the tent when the lawdog and Hannigan entered. One with an eye patch and beard sat at the makeshift desk, while the other, dressed in a knife-thrower's costume, stood beside it. Hannigan's gaze went to the daggers at the man's waist, then to the fellow who owned them. The man shifted feet, looked away, and the manhunter had no doubt this was the fellow who had tried to take his head off, different blades notwithstanding.

Vago looked up at the two, no expression on his face. He was the cooler of the two and Hannigan glimpsed a darkness in the man's eye he little cared for. He'd seen that look in the past, in the eyes of outlaws with nothing to lose and no moral compunction about what they did to reach their goals. Those men were the most dangerous, the ones who were like to make a stupid move without regard for the lives of anyone around them. The look vanished quickly, replaced by a smugness that was no improvement.

'Marshal Wentworth. I presume you've come to tell me you have arrested this man for the murder of Karlito?' Vago's tone came perfectly even, as if he'd requested coffee with his pie.

'I reckon that means you know who I am?' Hannigan said.

'Who else would you be?' Vago let a thin smile filter onto his lips.

'That ain't the reason I'm here,' the marshal said. 'Woman in town discovered her child missing this morning.'

Vago leaned back in his chair. 'And you figure he's here, before we even open for the day's business?' Still no expression change and Hannigan was having a hard time reading him. Here was a man who could play the game better than the run-of-the-mill outlaw he normally encountered.

The marshal stepped closer to the desk. 'She says he was hell-bent on seeing your circus. Looks like he might have snuck out last night to do so.'

Vago shook his head. 'I assure you,

Marshal, you won't find any children here at this hour. Furthermore, why is Mr Hannigan with you and not in a cell? I demand justice for poor Karlito.'

'Told you when we talked last night I got nothing to hold him on. He didn't have time to string up your employee. Dove places his entrance at just before nine and she followed him up the stairs not more than two minutes after he went up. Reckon whoever killed the dwarf was long gone by then.'

'Ah, Wild West impartiality at work,' Vago said, voice condescending. 'Lawmen stick together, don't they?'

'Carnie people don't?' countered the marshal, patience obviously wearing thin.

'Touché, Marshal. But again, you'll find no children in my circus. Now if you'll be so kind as to leave, Mr Ganado and I have the day's shows to prepare for.'

'You don't mind if we take a look around first, Mr Vago?' Hannigan said, folding his arms.

'Now just why would I allow that, Mr Hannigan? You are no more than a glorified killer from what I hear and have no right invading this circus's privacy.'

All the while Hannigan noticed Ganado growing increasingly antsy. The manhunter had been watching him out of the corner of his eye and noted the man definitely disliked the course the conversation was taking. He didn't want the grounds searched and that made the bounty hunter even more determined to do so.

Hannigan smiled a patronizing smile. 'I would think you would have as much interest as anyone in making sure that child isn't around here, Mr Vago.'

Vago's eye narrowed. 'And why would that be, Mr Hannigan?'

'Your business depends on folks coming around, bringing their young-uns. Reckon if word got out unfortunate circumstances had befallen some poor child at your show, they might stay away.'

'There's always the next town.' Vago

smiled, obviously enjoying what went unsaid between them. The carnival man was playing with him, daring him to accuse him outright.

'Let me put it to you a little more bluntly, Mr Vago. We don't get to look around these grounds and in those wagons and tents and I follow you night and day, to every town you head for, for as long as it takes.'

Ganado let out a muffled curse, but Vago didn't flinch.

'And Mr Hannigan will have company,' Marshal Wentworth added.

Vago sighed. 'It's always the same isn't it, Marshal?'

'What's that, Mr Vago?' The lawdog's tone had hardened, a measure of exasperation creeping in.

'For carnie folk. Oddities . . . freaks, if you will, as well as men of different color, different religions. Always the first to be suspected, the last to be exonerated. The ones most likely to be unduly persecuted, blamed.'

The marshal frowned. 'Save the

speech for when you run for office, Mr Vago. I ain't in the mood for it this time of day.'

Vago's face for the first time showed a glimmer of annoyance. 'Very well. I'll accompany you, but please make it quick. We do have a business to run here.'

Vago stood and motioned to Ganado to take over whatever paperwork he'd been concerned with. Ganado didn't look much like he wanted to stay behind but didn't put up a fight.

The search of the grounds was thorough and took about an hour. They roused the carnie workers and performers, Hannigan getting a look at the oddest collection of human beings he'd ever seen. Women with beards, the strong man who seemed unable to do more than glare, even a cage that contained what the sign proclaimed was a talking pig. Jezebel, the snake charmer, gave him a spiteful look that made him glad the marshal had taken the task of searching the serpent tent.

They had just finished looking into Madam Mystique's wagon. Tootie stood nearby, yawning, making sure not to give away her association with Hannigan by ignoring him. He felt a measure of relief at seeing she was OK, but didn't let it show on his face.

'As I told you, Marshal,' Vago said, as they stood outside the Gypsy's wagon. 'No children here.'

'What's in that wagon?' Hannigan indicated the plain cart next to the gypsy's. A padlock secured its doors.

Vago didn't miss a beat. 'It's a supply wagon, carries equipment, tents. It's empty at the moment.'

'Why's it locked, then?' asked Hannigan.

'To discourage runaway children from climbing into it,' Vago said, voice cold.

'Under the circumstances, Mr Vago,' the marshal said, 'that's not very goddamned funny.'

Vago smiled without humor. 'It was not meant to be.'

'Open it,' Hannigan said.

Vago eyed him, a glint of anger in his

gaze. 'I told you it was empty. Perhaps you would have better luck asking my fortune teller where your missing child is?'

The challenge was as direct as Vago could make it without coming right out and accusing Tootie of working with the manhunter.

'Like the man told you,' the marshal said. 'Open it.'

Vago sighed and took a key from his shirt pocket. Going to the wagon, he unlocked the padlock and pulled the doors open. The interior of the wagon was, as he had said, empty. Hannigan wasn't happy about it but there was no denying the obvious.

Vago closed the doors and relocked the wagon. 'Satisfied?'

The marshal nodded reluctantly.

'I figure we're done here, Hannigan,' the marshal said. 'There's no sign of the boy. I'll start checking the local fishing holes.'

Vago smiled an ingratiating smile and gave a slight bow. He turned and strode away from them.

Tootie, standing with her arms folded, didn't look at Hannigan until the owner was out of sight, then said in a quiet voice as she started up the steps into her wagon, 'Find him, Jim.'

Hannigan didn't acknowledge her words but the marshal glanced at him with a curious expression.

'She your girl?' he asked in a whisper.

Hannigan nodded. 'She's my girl.'

★   ★   ★

Back in the main tent, Ganado frowned and shifted feet as Vago came in. A hint of panic swam in his eyes and sweat beaded on his brow.

'You worry too goddamned much, Ganado,' Vago said. 'They didn't find a thing.'

'That was a damn poor idea takin' that kid while Hannigan's nosin' around here.'

'Couldn't be helped. We're being paid for three, I was two behind and he obligingly snuck in here.'

Ganado blew out a snort of disgust. 'You ain't foolin' me, Vago. You're playing a game with Hannigan. I know you too well not to see what's going on. You see him as a challenge, someone to better. I'm here to tell you, he ain't the guy you want to dance with.'

Vago smiled. 'I'm showing Mr Hannigan how weak he truly is, how powerless to save those he loves from their destiny.'

Ganado studied him a moment. 'You mean that gypsy girl, don't you? You know her from somewhere and you aim to take her from him. That ain't gonna happen, Vago. I know Hannigan's type and his type don't inspire turncoats.'

Vago's face turned a shade darker. 'She's . . . none of your concern.'

'He won't let that child's disappearance ride. I could see it in his eyes. He's got the look of a starved dog who won't give up a bone.'

'Then I reckon I best show him who's head of the pack.'

Ganado looked about ready to argue the point, but apparently thought better of it. 'No more kids till he's dealt with. Please, Vago? You'll get our necks stretched if you don't lay low.'

Vago laughed and walked back out into the daylight, leaving Ganado wishing he'd never hooked up with the sonofabitch, but knowing he had long passed the point of having any way out.

# 8

As the afternoon waned, Tootie breathed a sigh of discouragement. She had seen no sign of the missing child on the circus grounds after spending the better part of the day trying to be as inconspicuous as possible while searching for clues. The search convinced her that if Vago had abducted the child, he wasn't hiding him close by. But where else would he stash the boy?

She cut through an alley between two tents, frustrated with herself for coming up empty. She'd failed to get a chance at the safe in the main tent as well. Vago's second, Ganado, had stuck close to the place the entire day. The man gave her the willies, though in a different way than Vago. Ganado was the type of outlaw she was used to, a follower, more obviously crooked. She imagined Vago held tight rein on him.

Ganado had gone out of his way to ignore her, likely at Vago's order, except for covert looks of suspicion. Ganado was certain she was connected to Hannigan, in her estimation, and wasn't happy with Vago's plan to keep her near.

Exiting the alley, she wandered back towards her wagon, avoiding contact with the other circus folk wandering about. She'd surveyed most of them earlier, reaching the conclusion none were likely to betray their leader's confidence, especially after Karlito's murder.

Vago. She couldn't force away the feeling she knew him from somewhere. At times it almost surfaced, only to vanish when she tried to focus on it. If she didn't know better she would have sworn she was purposely suppressing the memory. It wasn't like her, but any thought of a past meeting with Vago disturbed her, made her want to flee from herself.

*What the devil's wrong with me?*

Growing more frustrated, her thoughts shifted to Hannigan. She wondered what he was doing, whether he had found any leads to the child. The notion made her wonder something else: what if she wanted a child of her own some day, a family, a life beyond tracking dangerous men and bringing them to justice? What if Hannigan saw her as only a partner, not a woman or a wife? It might have been old-fashioned in a changing world, but she couldn't help those feelings when she thought of him, when she thought of the family she'd never had.

No, that was wrong. She had experienced that family, but for too short a time. Vicious men had taken it from her and she'd been forced to grow up on her own. Forged by fire and survival, she'd never had the strength that came from the love and warmth of a family. She had a different strength, one she might never have discovered had the events of that day she'd watched her parents murdered never transpired.

She would have given anything to

have changed that day, but she'd long ago come to terms with the fact that she could not. God made choices sometimes, ones she couldn't possibly hope to fathom. She hoped He had His reasons and that they were worth it.

She'd given up trying to see any way they possibly could be. She'd given up screaming at His cruel Plan.

In vulnerable moments she longed for the grounding that came with a normal life, even more so since she met Hannigan.

But those thoughts were for the future. She didn't want a child now, not yet, but someday that would change. Would he feel the same way? Or would he give her excuses about men from his past tracking them down, threatening any serene life they tried to lead? He was a master of avoidance, but maybe she'd give him no choice. She wasn't without her methods.

She almost smiled. 'Maybe we'll start on that tonight, Mr Hannigan,' she whispered.

A sound penetrated her thoughts. It was low, a moan, maybe, like the sound a child in distress might make. She peered about, looking first at the opened doors of her wagon then at the plain locked cart near hers. Her gaze focused on it. If she hadn't known better she might have pegged the sound as coming from there, but Hannigan and the marshal had found that wagon empty. She strolled over to it, focusing on the lock, then peering along its side. Maybe she had simply imagined the sound. Her mind had been fixated on her search for the child and her own thoughts of a family.

Going to it, she drifted along the wagon's side, fingers absently dragging across its surface. She stopped, tapped on the panel. Listening, she heard nothing.

'Hello?' she said, voice just loud enough to be heard by someone in the wagon, but not anyone close by.

For a second she thought she heard another moan, but it was so slight and other noises of people milling about the circus made it impossible to be sure.

She knelt, peering beneath the wagon, examining its springs and iron tires, the wooden flooring.

'Looking for anything in particular?'

The voice belonged to a woman and came from behind her, nearly jumping her out of her skin. She straightened and turned to see the snake charmer standing in back of her. A small green snake enwrapped the woman's wrist. A peculiar look danced in her eyes. She was raking Tootie's body with a gaze that should have been reserved for a man.

'You normally come up on folks so quietlike?' Tootie said, gripping her nerves.

Jezebel shrugged. 'Wasn't all that quiet. You were . . . involved.'

'I lost a locket. Was looking under the wagons for it.'

'You figure it crawled on over there on its lonesome or do you just enjoy sitting under wagons?' The woman gave her a cutting smile. Tootie's mind fumbled for an excuse, but the woman took a step towards her before she could find one. 'Don't worry, sugar, I know what you were looking for. I doubt you'll find it under there, though.'

Tootie couldn't tell whether the girl really knew or she was just taunting her. 'I don't know what you mean.'

'All right, sugar, play it that way.' The woman leaned in and Tootie fought the urge to recoil. She didn't much care for snakes and she cared even less for this woman.

'I don't like snakes,' Tootie said, making the double meaning clear.

Jezebel smiled. Her free hand drifted up, the back of her fingers drifting over Tootie's cheek. 'You know, I ain't particular who I bed, Miss Fortune Teller. I could be real nice to you if you were nice to me.'

Tootie turned her face from the woman's touch. 'I don't go that way.'

'There's always a first time — '

'Jezebel!' A man's voice snapped from the front of the wagon.

The snake charmer jerked her hand away and peered at the figure of Avara Ganado coming up to them, annoyance in her gaze. Tootie wasn't sure whether to be relieved or more repulsed.

'You always ruin the moment, lover.' Jezebel, frowning, stroked her snake's head.

Ganado's eyes narrowed with anger. 'Just what the hell are you doing? Bad enough I gotta watch you with every damned thing in pants, now it's skirts?' From Ganado's tone Tootie could tell he'd caught this woman in this position more than once in the past and he figured her for his property.

'Relax, sugar. Maybe we could all do it together.' Jezebel giggled and fury jumped into Ganado's eyes. His hand snapped up, the back of it taking the snake charmer hard across her right cheek. Jezebel's head rocked and she let out a small cry.

The snake charmer peered at him,

eyes narrowed. 'You want it rough, sugar, we can do that, too.'

'Get the hell back to your tent.' Ganado's voice came low, demanding. 'I'll deal with you later.'

Jezebel didn't move, simply glared at him. Then she let out a chopped laugh. 'One of these days, sugar, you won't be treatin' me that way.' Tootie suddenly wondered if any of the woman's snakes were poisonous.

'I'll treat you any goddamned way I want. And I catch you with anyone again it'll be the last time.'

Jezebel gave him a glare, then cast another at Tootie. 'Ask your little gypsy whore what she was doing looking around this wagon, lover.' The woman flashed Tootie a spiteful sneer, then walked away, disappearing around the end of the wagon. Tootie wondered if things were about to go from bad to worse.

Ganado peered at her, face two shades redder than it been a moment before. 'What the hell is she talking about?'

'I was looking for my locket. I lost it.'

'Go back to your own wagon and take my advice, curiosity ain't a welcome or healthy thing with carnie folk.'

She had the notion to ask him which pulp novel he'd stolen that line from but caught herself before making the situation worse than it already was.

She felt his gaze on her as she went back to her wagon and climbed the stairs. The perfect end to the perfect day, she reckoned, cursing Ganado and the bitch of a snake charmer. She hoped Hannigan was having better luck.

\* \* \*

If Jim Hannigan had gotten any luck today he reckoned it was all bad. He and the marshal had searched every nook and cranny of that circus for the missing boy and something the size of a child wasn't easy to hide. That made him wonder just what Vago could have done with him. It was possible the child had just wandered off somewhere and wound up in trouble, but it appeared too coincidental and he wasn't a man who liked coincidence. That meant Vago had stashed the boy somewhere else. But where?

As he walked along the boardwalk, the late-afternoon sun sinking towards the distant mountains, he struggled to keep his mood from growing more somber. The case was frustrating him. He didn't like Vago or Ganado and he didn't like Tootie risking her life working for them. Usually he felt fairly confident in her cover — whether he liked it or not was another thing — but in this case Vago knew her part, and was watching her. Beyond that, Vago was a different breed than they were used to, more dangerous in his estimation. He was brazen, taunting. Not only had he taken the child right under Hannigan's nose, but somehow he had managed to avoid Tootie's watchful eye. Hannigan hoped the brazenness would lead to a reckless move, but waiting around for it was making him edgy.

'Hannigan.' The voice came from behind him, and he stopped, turning to see the marshal stepping from his office.

'Marshal.' Jim said, certain by the look of frustration on the lawdog's face he hadn't found any clue to the missing boy, either.

'I searched the local fishing holes and any place that might interest a boy that age, but came up empty-handed.'

Hannigan nodded. 'Figured as much. Nothing on my end, either. What the hell did they do with him?'

'We can't be sure it *was* them. At least not until we get something more definite.'

Hannigan's face tightened. 'It was them. You see how nervous Ganado was when we were questioning them? He was worried we'd find something.'

The marshal scratched his chin. 'But there was nothing there to find.'

Hannigan sighed. 'I know. But if there's a chance that kid's still alive we've got to keep trying.'

'Seems I got some small print to add to the page, however.'

Hannigan cocked an eyebrow. ' 'Bout the child?'

'No, jewelry. Farnswell at the jewelry store said some of his gems went missing. He noticed it this morning when he opened up for business. Some necklaces and bracelets, all items with precious stones.'

'Vago had a busy night.'

'Farnswell said he didn't recall any strangers in the store, and we didn't find any missing jewelry when we searched the tents and wagons this morning, neither.'

'I noticed a large safe in the main tent, or any one of those carnie folks might have had the pieces on their person. Jewelry's a lot easier to hide than a child.'

'Way I figured it, too. I thought of heading over there and forcing Vago to open his safe, but it's likely a waste of time.'

Hannigan nodded, looking off in the direction of the circus. 'By now it could be anywhere. It's small, transportable. If Vago had it in his safe temporarily, he sure as hell would figure you'd come lookin' and wouldn't leave it there.'

The marshal nodded. 'My thoughts.'

Hannigan's gaze shifted as he noticed a woman coming towards them, recognizing her as the mother from this morning. When she reached them he saw her face was more haggard, looking years older than earlier in the day. Dark pouches nested beneath her eyes and redness from crying nearly obscured the whites.

'Please tell me you found him, Marshal,' she said, voice pleading, fragile. A knot twisted in Hannigan's belly.

'Sorry, ma'am, we haven't. We searched the circus and I scoured the area around town. Hate to say it, but I'm afraid there's nothing else we can do at the moment.'

The marshal said it with as much softness in his voice as possible but the woman appeared as if all life had drained from her. She staggered, on the verge of collapse, and Hannigan reached out to steady her. She gazed up at him with wide eyes filled with pain.

'Please, Mr Hannigan, do something. Please . . . '

He wanted to tell her everything would be all right, that her son would come home to her happy and safe and make her life the pleasant hell that only little boys were capable of, but the words wouldn't come. He couldn't give her false hope, not when the other missing children had never been found and without a shred of evidence to indicate what Vago had done with him.

'I'm sorry, ma'am. I truly am.' He searched for something, anything to comfort her. 'I'll keep looking, I give you my word.'

She sniffled, fighting to steady herself. 'I . . . suppose that's the most I can ask. You've been kind, Mr Hannigan. I just don't know where else to turn.'

He tried to smile, but there wasn't much heart in it. 'I'll see you home, ma'am. Best you wait there while we work this out in case he should come back. And try to get yourself some rest. You won't be any good to him if you fret yourself into the ground.'

She nodded and he put his arm around her, guiding her back down the boardwalk, the marshal's head hanging as he watched them go.

An hour later Hannigan headed back to town, passing the circus on his way in, debating whether he should just storm in there and beat the hell out of Vago until the man admitted his crimes and told him what had become of the boy.

*Get hold of yourself, Hannigan. Anger won't do you or that child any good.*

He had to let his years of trail-honed instinct take over, guide him the way it had successfully in the past.

After a quick dinner of beans and bacon washed down with coffee at the café, he spent the next few hours questioning the jewelry shop owner to no avail and scouring the room at the saloon where he'd discovered the body of the dwarf for clues. He found nothing and though it was what he expected, his discouragement jumped another notch. He questioned some of the doves and barkeep, hoping one of them might be able to place a carnie worker anywhere near the saloon near the time of the killing, but whoever hanged Karlito might as well have been a ghost.

He had just started back towards his hotel room when he noticed someone following him.

Night had come to Angel Pass and with it a chill. Hanging lanterns burned outside some of the shops, amber light mingling with shadow, marbling the rutted streets. From the circus the sounds of a calliope drifted over the breeze, along with shouts and cheers. A glow buttered the night from that direction, from torches burning about the grounds.

A slight scuffing sound reached his ear, making his manhunter's sixth sense tingle. Pausing in front of the hotel, he pretended to glance back towards the saloon, as if considering returning to the drinkerie for another round. From the corner of his eye he caught movement, someone ducking into an ally. He didn't get a good look at the man, but wagered the tracker had to be connected to Vago. Vago either had decided to track Hannigan back to where he was staying or put a watch on him.

The manhunter pressed his back to the wall of the hotel and moved towards the alley, keeping against the buildings and making no sound.

When Hannigan reached a shop that flanked the alley, he paused, waiting.

It didn't take long before a head poked around the corner, peering in the direction of the hotel.

'Evenin',' Hannigan said and the man let out a strangled squawk.

The manhunter spun from the wall and grabbed two handfuls of the man's denim shirt, hauling him out of the alley and up onto the boardwalk. Traces of white and red theatrical make-up stained the man's startled face. Hannigan jerked him close.

'I don't care much for clowns,' he said, then hurled the man over a hitch rail running along the boardwalk. The man landed in a trough with a splash, arms and legs flailing in a mad scramble to get back out.

Hannigan leaped over the rail and landed beside the trough as the man, dripping water, came to his feet. He sent a punch down the pike that clacked against the stalker's jaw with a sound like two blocks colliding. The man flew over backwards, crashing onto the hard-pack, but recovered fast enough to roll onto his side and spring back up to his feet.

The move told Hannigan the fellow

was likely an acrobat of some sort, used to taking falls.

The stalker flung himself at Hannigan, arms flying with no particular skill or direction. Hannigan's hat flew to the ground and the attacker increased his flurry of swings.

A knee slammed into Hannigan's thigh; welts of pain radiated up and down his leg. The manhunter retaliated with a sharp uppercut, but the assailant jerked his head left with perfect timing, avoiding the blow.

The attacker winged a fist at Hannigan. The manhunter sidestepped, avoiding the blow, but got caught with a second fist to his bread basket thrown only a beat behind the first. The blow sent pain through his belly and wind burst from his lungs. He fought a surge of nausea.

The attacker had switched from wild to precise, taking Hannigan off guard, which was no doubt what he intended.

The manhunter, half-doubled, shuffled back a couple feet, cursing himself for using less caution than he should have.

The man charged at him again, likely believing Hannigan to be stunned enough to finish off.

The manhunter exploded upward with a vicious blow to the man's chin. He'd had the hell beaten out of him too many times on recent cases and he'd be damned if this was going to be another of them.

The attacker staggered. Hannigan wasted no time following up. He jabbed a blow to the man's nose and heard a satisfying crack, felt liquid spurt across his knuckles.

The man cursed and swung. Although he had the skill of an acrobat he didn't have Hannigan's size and strength. The blow glanced from Hannigan's shoulder, doing no damage. The manhunter snapped an uppercut; bone hit bone; the man's jaw changed shape and he collapsed.

The attacker groaned, rolling onto his side, blood streaming from his nose and mouth.

Hannigan squatted, grabbing the man's shirt and jerking his face close. 'You go back to your boss and tell him he best do better than you if he expects to take me on, you hear? Tell him it's only a matter of time till I find out what he did with that boy. Tell him he sends anyone else after me I'll send him back in a box next time.'

Hannigan slammed the man back to the dirt, then straightened and retrieved his hat from the street, setting it on his head.

Going to the trough, he washed the blood from his knuckles while keeping an eye on the man, who struggled to his feet, then headed off in the direction of the circus, the man making no attempt to conceal his destination.

Hannigan went back to his hotel, wondering what Vago's next move would be after he discovered his man had failed at whatever mission he'd been sent on. Would he strike at Hannigan again soon or possibly move out the circus early? The law had nothing solid against him, could not stop his band from pulling stakes, and if he cut his losses now, they had a clear path out of Angel Pass. From there they could lay low for a spell. Hannigan could follow them to their next destination, but that was time-consuming and every moment they ran free lessened the chances of finding that missing boy.

Coming from his thoughts, Hannigan entered the hotel. The night manager gave him a peculiar smile, but the man-hunter ignored it and climbed the stairs leading to his room. Going down the hall, he stopped before his door.

A sound from within his room made him hesitate. The sound was peculiar, like . . . water trickling?

He was pretty certain Vago had sent his man to learn which hotel he was staying at and wouldn't have another waiting in his room. He knew only one person with a knack for getting through locked doors without difficulty.

He opened the door, expecting to

find Tootie sitting in a chair or on the edge of the bed, but the moment he saw her he froze where he was standing. His mouth dropped open.

A soft amber glow pervaded the room, coming from a half-dozen candles flickering on the bureau top. In the center of the room was an oblong tin tub and in it sat Tootie, arms draped over either side. Her dark hair, pinned atop her head with errant wisps cork-screwing to either side of her face, shimmered with jewels of amber from the candlelight. Her mahogany eyes glistened with a smoky lust that sent shivers down his spine. The air carried a delicate scent, rosewater, if he reckoned right.

'You gonna close the door or just wait till everybody sees my business?' She cocked an eyebrow and for a moment he swore someone had nailed his feet to the floor.

Overcoming a measure of his spell, he doffed his hat and tossed it onto a chair, while easing the door shut behind him. He suddenly had no idea where to look, his gaze going to the wall, the floor, anywhere but at the girl in the tub. Not that he didn't have a powerful urge to gaze at her nakedness, but a shred of nervous chivalry compelled him to turn away.

'Um, I thought you were at the circus?' Was his voice shaking? Damn. Now his hands were, too.

She drew a leg out of the water, ran her fingers sensually along both sides of her calf. His knees nearly buckled. 'I snuck out after my last show. Closed up my wagon, made sure that snake woman was nowhere around, then came here. Figured a warm bath was just the thing for a cold autumn night. The hotel man charged me an arm and a leg for it this late at night.'

'That explains the look he gave me when I came in.'

'Bet it was nothin' like the look on your face when you opened that door a minute ago.' She giggled. He didn't think it was quite that funny.

He swallowed, having a hell of a time controlling the desire flooding him. He gazed at her, struggling not to look at anything below her neck, but it was suddenly the hardest thing he'd ever done.

'What are you doing, Tootie?'

'Taking a bath. That should be pretty obvious.' Her voice came low, sultry. She was doing it on purpose, and it made his heart stutter.

'I mean, besides takin' a bath.'

'OK, call it taking the bull by the horns.' She rose from the water, standing in the tub, revealing herself to him and he had no chance to look away. He couldn't have had he wanted to. Rivulets of water streamed down her skin, which glowed with flame light until it appeared to be made of liquid honey.

He let out some sort of sound; he wasn't entirely certain what it was but it came with a sudden flush of heat to his face and weakness to his knees.

'Well, don't you have anything to say,

Mr Hannigan?' Her words came with a buttery softness that sent shivers cascading through his body.

'Uh, you're a little more knock-kneed than I figured you for . . . '

Her eyes narrowed. 'Jim Hannigan, that's got to be the stupidest thing you've ever come out with and I got a long list to compare it to!'

She was right and he knew it was idiotic the moment he said it, but suddenly he had little control over his emotions or his words. The sight of her beauty did something to him he couldn't even begin to figure out. What he felt now he would have thought impossible. Waves of desire, warmth, unlike anything he'd ever experienced, even with Catherine, the woman he once thought he loved. Angela del Pelado was mesmerizing, the loveliest creature he'd ever laid eyes upon. Every fiber of his being wanted her, screamed for her, and any thoughts of resisting dissolved before they could be formed.

'You're . . . beautiful . . . ' he whispered.

She smiled, pink rosing her cheeks and emotion burning raw in her eyes. 'There's a towel on that other chair. I reckon I'm getting a mite chilled standing here in my altogether.'

He nodded, licking his lips, then fetched the towel. As she stepped out of the tub he wrapped it about her, drying her off. Her scent intoxicated him. She pressed into his arms and he let the towel drop. Her lips met his, soft, with a taste as sweet and inviting as a summer peach. For a moment he lost himself completely, and every suppressed emotion came bursting out, flooding his being, overwhelming his senses. As if every lost dream of his lifetime came alive and was fulfilled in this moment.

She pulled back slightly, their lips a fraction of space apart. 'I'm not giving you a choice anymore, Jim Hannigan. Tonight I'm makin' you mine.'

'I'm already yours. Reckon I was the moment I met you.'

★　★　★

Two hours later they lay beneath the covers, the candles doused, the room shimmering darkness. Her breath whispered against his chest and her body pressed warm to his. What he'd just experienced, what they'd experienced together, was something he thought only existed in fairytales or for others. Not for a man named Jim Hannigan, a man destined to be alone. It brought a jumble of confused feelings and thoughts but he refused to dwell on them, because for this moment, for this night, there was only the woman lying beside him.

'I really wanted to find him . . . ' she whispered, breaking the silence.

'Your brother?'

'Yes. I thought . . . stupidly, I reckon, Aunt Agnes would tell me he had grown up with them, was somewhere close by, maybe even in Angel Pass. That maybe he thought his sister had gone forever, but I would show up and just surprise him, throw my arms around him and tell him everything was going to be OK now because we had our family back. I knew better. I knew how Agnes would react. But it didn't stop me from having this simple-minded delusion that for once God would see to it things worked out for me instead of leaving me to be tossed on the wind. But that won't happen now. I'll never find him and things won't ever be the way I dreamed they would. It hurts.'

Emotion clutched in his throat. 'I promise you I'll turn hell upside down looking for him, Tootie.'

He felt a tear drip onto his chest.

'I know you will, but we have nowhere to start. He's gone. I have to face it.'

'I could talk to your aunt. Maybe she'd be more open with a stranger.'

'Wouldn't do any good. She was telling me the truth, I'm sure of it. He's . . . a boy on his own . . . doubtful he'd survive . . . '

'You survived.'

'I was in a home. He was on his own.'

She went silent a moment, her breathing heavy, another tear hitting his chest. 'I wish I could remember more about him, but I was so young . . . '

She hesitated and he felt her shudder in his arms. 'What's wrong?'

'I . . . don't know. I just felt a chill or something. For a moment I couldn't even see his face in my mind anymore.'

'We'll find him, Tootie, if he's to be found.'

'You can't promise me that, Jim.'

'No, just that I'll do my damnedest.'

'I love you, Jim Hannigan.'

The words came like velvet and sent a wave of shivers through him. He must have frozen for longer than he thought because Tootie suddenly thumped a fist against his chest and even in the darkness he could see her peering at him with an annoyed expression.

'I . . . love you, too . . . ' he whispered.

For the first night Jim Hannigan could recollect, he slept without the faces of any of the men he'd killed invading his dreams. He wasn't even certain what woke him, but the room was brighter because the moon had risen and alabaster light bled through the window. He saw her standing there, next to the window, gazing out into the waning night. She had dressed in her gypsy clothing and a strange longing for her flooded his being, though she hadn't left him yet.

'I have to get back, Jim,' she said, voice low. 'I almost wish I had waited until we weren't on a case because I don't want to leave you ever again. But I couldn't wait. I kept thinking if anything ever happened to one of us . . . well, I didn't want to go to my Maker never having shared your bed.'

He pushed himself up to his elbows, the familiar worry coming over him. 'Don't go back. I sent a man who followed me back to Vago last night. I practically dared Vago to make a move. Whatever his game is the stakes just went up.'

'I have to, Jim. Those children, that

boy, we've got to find him.'

'It's too dangerous now.'

She uttered a humorless laugh. 'It's *always* been dangerous. But you know I can't change the way I am, any more than you can change your way. Least for now.' She went to him and leaned over, kissing him deeply. A moment later she had slipped out into the hallway and closed the door behind her.

The room suddenly felt achingly empty. His life felt empty. It wasn't, it was more complete than it had ever been and the memory of their night together was one he'd go to his grave recollecting and savoring.

'You've just run out of excuses, Hannigan,' he whispered. 'Now what do you do?'

# 9

Dawn painted the horizon in chilled rose by the time Tootie reached the circus grounds. The night's coolness lingered and she wished she had worn more than just the gypsy's get-up to shield her from it. With a shiver, she hugged herself, gooseflesh rising on her arms and shoulders. Frost crunched beneath her high-laced shoes as she hurried towards her wagon.

Last night had been the most wonderful of her life. It had filled her with feelings and sensations she'd never dreamed possible for a woman who'd spent most of her life alone, dedicated to her mission, driven by the suppressed rage and craving for justice inadvertently instilled within her by the killers who took her parents' lives. The things most women took for granted — love, hope, raising a family — were not for that lost little girl who for years had dreamed only in the color of blood. But with one night of passion, of the touching of souls, everything had changed. Those things were possible now for that lost little girl, because she was lost no longer.

Her decision to force the issue with Hannigan had worked out better than she might have dreamed. She had taken a chance exposing herself — in more ways than one — to him. Yet at the same time small doubts plagued her mind: Maybe he'd just been caught up in a moment of lust and desire and would change his mind once he came to his senses; maybe he didn't really mean the three words he'd said, the ones that replaced the fire of rage inside her with the blaze of love.

*You're being foolish!* she assured herself. He meant those words; she had heard it in his voice and a man like Jim Hannigan never said things he didn't mean. Maybe that in itself frightened her more than she thought it would, because it meant she now had everything to lose and a lifetime to gain.

'You've just risked the whole pot,' she whispered. No bluff, no aces, just blind faith. It felt terrifying; it felt wonderful.

She came from her thoughts as she reached her wagon and paused at the doors. Putting aside her worries and hopes, she sighed, gaze drifting to the main tent in the distance. Her mission — *their* mission. That had to be settled first. She needed a clue to the whereabouts of those missing children. The tent was likely deserted at this time of the morning, giving her the perfect opportunity to get a look at the contents of that safe. The move was risky, because she wasn't certain what time Vago or Ganado rose, but she had to chance it. Vago was being too careful around her and after failing to frame Hannigan he might decide to pull stakes. She had to act now, before they lost all chance of recovering that boy. She knew she could open nearly any safe in a few moments time, so the sooner she got started, the lower the odds of getting caught.

She glanced about, making sure the sleazy snake charmer or any of the carnies were nowhere to be seen, then glided towards the main tent, avoiding frosted-coated leaves and spots of thin ice in an effort to make as little noise as possible. In the dawn hush every footstep seemed exaggeratedly loud and her heart started to beat faster.

Reaching the tent, she slipped around to the back, locating the rear flap. It was tied down and it took her a moment to get the bottom open wide enough for her to fit through. Glancing back to make sure nobody saw her, she went in.

Gloom pervaded the interior, and she waited a moment for her eyes to adjust.

She went to the makeshift desk, grabbing the lantern there and the box of lucifers next to it.

She carried the lamp to the safe and brought it to light, turning the flame just low enough to see the safe dial but to remain unnoticeable from the outside the tent.

As she knelt beside the safe, she stopped and peered behind her, a slight sound reaching her ears.

A heartbeat. Two. Silence.

The eerie stillness rattled her nerves. Likely it had been nothing more than the breeze rustling a brittle leaf, but she waited another moment just in case. She fought to steady her hand, which she noticed was quivering now. Maybe it was just this case, or maybe it was something submerged within her memory, but she couldn't recollect ever having felt this jittery when it came to doing her job. It wasn't like her. She relied on strength, guile, confidence and skill. For the first time since that day her aunt sent her to the home she felt as if she had had damn little of any of those traits.

Sighing, she pressed her ear against the safe door; the chilled metal gave her a shiver. The dial was frigid, which made getting the feel of it through her fingertips more difficult and a little uncomfortable. Her breath steamed out as she eased the dial around and her heart pounded in her ears. The clicking sound made by the tumblers seemed magnified in the frosty silence.

It took longer than it normally would have to find the first number, 30. The safe was modern, sturdy and well-designed, a type she had never opened. She reckoned if that home her aunt had sent her to had been good for anything, it had provided her with the opportunity to practice getting into locked rooms and closed safes. Not that the folks running the home much appreciated that talent, but she had never been one for their prescribed daily routines of sewing and knitting, so what was a girl left alone in her room supposedly reading to do if not hone the skills she might need later in life?

She noticed the interior of the tent lightening; dawn was brightening to morning fast. Time was running out and each second that passed meant a greater chance of getting caught.

She got the second number — 22. Despite the cold, sweat beaded on her brow. She swallowed at the tightness gripping her throat.

Fifteen minutes dragged by, fifteen minutes she really couldn't afford to let pass.

*It's taking too long . . .*

A measure of frustration trickled into her veins. This was no simple lock. The safe was the most complicated she'd encountered and the doubt she could even figure out the final number niggled her mind. Normally, she would have used the sawbones' stethoscope she'd appropriated on a case she kept in her portmanteau, but she'd reckoned she wouldn't need her equipment on this case and had left the bag back in the office. She regretted that decision now.

Ten more minutes went by. The tent interior lightened enough for her to douse the lantern.

Five more minutes.

*Dammit!*

A brittle click sounded. Grasping the

handle, she pulled open the door and blew out a sigh of relief. The interior contained two compartments, each piled with a number of papers, but no jewels. She reached inside, rummaged through the papers as neatly but quickly as she could manage. Her hands shook and the muscles in her shoulders ached with tension.

*You're taking too big a risk —*

Someone grabbed both her arms before she could even let out a sound and hoisted her to her feet, then heaved her over the makeshift desk. She hit the desk top hard, kept going, rolling over the opposite side then slamming into the ground hard enough to jolt the breath from her lungs. She saw boots coming towards her and struggled to get up, but couldn't make her body work fast enough to avoid the heel that crashed into her jaw.

Pain splintered through her chin and teeth and stars exploded before her eyes. Blackness swirled at the corners of her mind.

Another kick into her side lifted her up and over and deposited her onto her back. Stunned, she stared up at the tent ceiling, which shimmered and blurred before her vision. Distant voices echoed her ears, harsh, damning, male.

'I told you it was a goddamn mistake letting her get too close!' She recognized Ganado's tone and tried to focus, clear her head.

'We don't know what she was up to yet.' Vago's voice. Her senses cleared some as pain took over. Her jaw throbbed; she'd be lucky if it weren't broken. She struggled to sit up, saw the two men standing next to the desk, glaring down at her.

Ganado scoffed. 'She broke into the safe, for chrissakes! How much more proof you need that she's working with Hannigan?'

Vago peered at her, remained silent for a moment. 'She's got skills. Maybe we can bring her aboard.'

Tootie managed to get to her hands and knees. Grabbing the corner of the desk, she pulled herself up, leaning heavily against the board. Ganado made a move towards her, obviously intending to knock her from her feet again, but Vago stopped him.

Ganado spat. 'She's working with that manhunter. No way she'd go against him. She's not one of us, Vago. She never will be.'

'She might keep quiet.' Vago's eye settled on her and she suppressed the urge to shrink back. Blood dribbled from the corner of her mouth and she brushed it away with the back of her hand.

Ganado shook his head. 'Like hell! You don't know her. You can't trust her.'

Vago's expression didn't change. 'I know her.'

'What?' Ganado looked at his boss, shock on his face. 'How?'

Vago didn't answer him. Instead, he peered at Tootie. 'Join us, Hannah. We could use a woman with your talents.'

Tootie glared at him, defiant. 'And

those kids you take?'

He shrugged. 'They're weak. We do them a favor, make them strong. We get good money for them.'

'What becomes of them?' She had a feeling the answer was going to be one that would haunt her nightmares for the rest of her life.

'The organization we deal with sells them to Mex farmers, where they are used as labor. Some go to men of peculiar tastes. Whichever way they go they are shown how the world really is, made stronger.'

She swallowed, fury seething in her belly. 'They aren't made stronger. You destroy them.'

Vago shook his head, face grim. 'It made me stronger, Hannah. All my life I was passed around, forced to work for men no boy should ever have been near, forced to do things that were . . . unnatural. I was forged in the fires of hell. I learned to be strong, bleed every drop of weakness from my soul.'

'You're a monster!' She spat. Saliva

dribbled down his face. He brushed it away with the back of his hand.

'I'm a realist. The world is changing, and the weak perish. I survived because of what was done to me and I'll go on surviving.'

Ganado folded his arms, eyes narrowing. 'She won't join us, Vago. She'll run right back to Hannigan and bring him down on us. You heard what Jenkins said when he got back last night. Hannigan won't let this rest and next time he'll find that kid.'

Vago went silent. Darkness drifted across his face. Disgust rose like bile in Tootie's throat. In that moment, she wanted to kill Vago and Ganado. For once she understood how Hannigan felt when he made certain some of the men he went after never reached trial. Vago was evil made flesh. She'd witnessed depravity in outlaws, had seen men who abused or took advantage of others, but Vago, Vago's soul was black as the Devil's heart. And something deep inside her struggling to break free made her infinitely sad at the revelation.

Vago's face appeared momentarily grieved and she wondered just what he was thinking, why a man like him would hesitate.

When Vago spoke, his voice came low, hard, remorseless. 'We'll move out today. Send Armir after Hannigan. Tell him to make sure that manhunter never comes back here. You take care of the marshal yourself. We don't need any witnesses.'

'What about her?' Ganado ducked his chin towards Tootie.

Vago looked back to Tootie and again a hint of sadness flicked across his features. 'There's a stream outside of town, surrounded by a number of quicksand bogs. I noticed it when we rode in. Tie her up and throw her in the wagon. We'll drop her in a bog on our way out.' He smiled a grim smile at the shocked look on her face. 'Tooties don't float . . . '

It came crashing in on her then, every dark thought she had been

194

suppressing, every hint she had taken in and somehow refused deep in her subconscious to believe. Horror flooded her face and she slowly shook her head.

'No . . . ' she muttered, bile surging into her throat. She forced it down, fought to steady herself. She was strong, she told herself, she was strong and could face a truth she might have realized all along.

Ganado looked at Vago, uncomprehending. The circus man's grim expression strengthened. 'You asked how I knew her . . . Meet my sister, Angela, Ganado.'

'Alejandro . . . ' Tootie whispered, struggling to get her voice to work.

Alejandro del Pelado uttered a thin laugh. 'Not anymore . . . What happened to you, little sister? You've let weakness corrupt you, make you soft. I am doing those children a service. I'm doing the world a service.'

'You're deluded, Alejandro. I know what Agnes and Harker did was wrong. I know they never tried to find you but to become this . . . '

He smiled. 'I found *them*. I found them the same day you did. I made them pay for sending you away, for taking advantage of my weakness. Don't you see, I couldn't do anything to stop them then because I was weak, because they *made* me weak. But now I can, and I did.'

'They're . . . dead?' The truth grieved her more than it should have. They had never wanted her, never cared about a lost little girl or her brother, but somehow that little girl had cared about them in some buried part of her memory and still did.

'Join us, Tootie, learn to be strong, to let no one ever take advantage of you again, to let no one force you to do what you never wanted to do.'

Her mahogany eyes narrowed, fury a storm within them. 'I'll never join you, you sonofabitch. You're not the boy I recollected. You *were* strong, then. You used to protect me, teach me. What happened to you turned you into a ghoul. You've gone insane, Alejandro.

You no longer know the difference between strength and weakness, between right and wrong. Your past has blinded you. Your rage consumed you.'

Vago stared at her for dragging moments and she saw the darkness behind that gaze, the cyclone of fury and pain ... and something else, soullessness, an emptiness that told her the boy who was once her brother could no longer be reached.

After what seemed an eternity, Vago glanced at Ganado. 'Get her out of here.'

Ganado grabbed her arms and she struggled, kicking at his shins and trying to jerk free of his grip, but she was still weak from the blows, barely capable of staying on her feet. 'Bastard!' she screamed at her brother, tears flooding her eyes, despite her best efforts to keep them at bay. Everything she had ever believed about her brother, every memory of him, was now a lie, just another of God's twisted jokes.

Anger and pain sent a burst of

strength surging through her veins. She tried to jam a knee into Ganado's groin. The second cursed and struggled to hold her at a safe distance while pulling her towards the back flap. She dug her heels into the hardpack, did her best to sink her teeth into his forearm.

His fist hit the back of her head. Bursts of light exploded before her vision and she staggered, legs threatening to go in two different directions.

Ganado delivered a clubbing blow to her temple. The last thing she saw was the ground rushing up to meet her.

# 10

With the dawn Jim Hannigan was dressed and staring out the window into the brightening street below. A few shop owners headed for their establishments to prepare for the day's business while a handful of others wandered towards the café. Another early riser, using a broom handle, jabbed at a coating of ice in a trough. Frost glazed the corners of the hotel window, starting to melt as morning sunlight warmed the air.

He wished he hadn't let Tootie go back to that circus, but knew he couldn't have stopped her. He had no right to. She was her own woman and they were on a case. And since last night had closed any chance of ever going back to the way things were before he met her, he just had to adjust. That was the price, and with their consummation he had agreed to pay it.

A half-hour passed. Frost turned to liquid crystal, streaking down the glass. He considered heading to the café for breakfast, but the more he thought of Tootie at that carnival the more antsy he became. One child was already missing. Jewels had vanished. And Vago knew damn well Tootie was not whom she claimed to be.

Add that to his lack of headway on the case and a man used to action was likely to come right out of his skin. He banged a fist against the wall, frustration getting the better of him. He wasn't one for hanging his spurs over a bedpost. But what choice did he have? He either waited until Vago made another move, one that might endanger another child or Tootie, or let Tootie try to find something tangible he could bring to the law. If he tried to squeeze Vago, the man might pull stakes and his options would melt like the window frost. A boy's life would be forfeit.

To make matters worse, he reckoned

the original Madam Mystique would be released due to lack of evidence any moment now and come running back to Vago. When the gypsy recognized Tootie her already thin chances of finding what they did with the boy would evaporate.

Jim Hannigan went to the bed and plucked his hat from the post. Being cooped up in this room wasn't doing his disposition any good, and though he had little appetite, he'd go to the café and at least force down some coffee.

Setting his hat on his head, he skirted the tub, and went to the door.

Opening the door, he froze as he came face to face with a man who stood on the threshold, filling the doorway like a grinning grizzly. Hannigan instantly recognized the giant as the strongman from the carnival, Armir. A wild look glittered in his dark eyes and Hannigan got no chance to recover his composure before the strongman lunged at him.

Armir grabbed Hannigan by the shirt and heaved him backwards into the room. With a searing welt of agony, Hannigan's back slammed into the rim of the metal tub and the giant forced the manhunter's shoulders and head beneath the water.

Hannigan pried at the man's grip but couldn't break Armir's iron hold.

He'd managed only a gasped half-breath before going under and the struggle quickly used up the oxygen in his lungs. They began to ache and his mouth came open reflexively. Water flooded in, filled his sinuses with needles of pain.

A dark blotch that was the strong-man's face loomed before his water-blurred vision. Hannigan made a desperate attempt to jab his fingertips into the man's eyes, throat and nostrils but had little success. Armir simply pulled his head back and held Hannigan straight-armed beneath the water.

Things started to grow fuzzy at the edges of his mind. He was conscious of himself choking, struggling on pure instinct, a cascade of thoughts whirling through his head.

*You're going to die, Hannigan. In another moment you'll black out and Tootie will be next if they haven't killed her already —*

A burst of panic surged through him at the thought and he redoubled his efforts to break the strongman's grip. His arms knifed between Armir's, slamming into the bigger man's forearms with as much power as he could muster. In nearly the same move, the manhunter's knee snapped up, connecting with the strong man's vitals.

Armir's grip loosened suddenly and even beneath the water Hannigan heard a roar of pain come from the strongman. The manhunter surged upward, bursting from the water and twisting. He rolled over the side of the tub onto the floor, choking, gasping, his entire body trembling. On instinct, vision blurred, he kept rolling until he slammed into a wall. Streaming water, he forced himself to his feet, wobbly, the room whirling. He blinked, managed to get some of his breath back. His vision cleared and he saw the strongman straightening from a doubled-over position, fury on his face.

'You and that marshal should have left things alone, manhunter,' the giant said, voice like a bear rumbling from deep within a cave. 'Your nose don't belong in carnie business.'

Armir fumbled at his waist as he came towards Hannigan. The strong-man pulled a small-bladed knife from a sheath at his belt and Hannigan could see it was already coated with crimson. Had the giant gone after the marshal first?

He didn't have time to think on it. He side-stepped as the giant jerked up an arm, then plunged the knife towards Hannigan's chest.

The man was powerful, but not quick. With a loud *thuck*, the knife buried itself in the wall to the hilt.

Hannigan snapped a fist against the giant's ribs. He heard a satisfying crack, but the strongman didn't miss a beat.

Armir released the knife and made a

grab for the manhunter's shirt again. Hannigan avoided the clutch, launched another blow that slammed into the giant's chin. Armir's head rocked but the blow barely slowed him. He made another grab for Hannigan. The man-hunter dove, hitting the floor in a tumble and coming back to his feet halfway across the room, legs still shaky, breath beating out. He knew he'd never best the giant in a fight. It wouldn't be long before he tired and Armir would crush him. He had to even the odds somehow.

The strongman lunged towards him. Hannigan's hand swept to the Peace-maker at his hip, brought it up.

Armir, moving faster than Hannigan expected, grabbed the manhunter before he could level the gun and hoisted him clean off the floor. A malicious grin on his face, the strongman hauled him towards the window, obviously intending to hurl him through to the street two stories below.

Hannigan jerked up the sawed-off

Peacemaker in a crisp arc, clacking the man's chin.

Armir staggered a step, but recovered quickly. Hannigan swung again, putting as much strength behind the blow as he could. Metal contacted bone with a sound like a hammer and anvil colliding. Armir paused, eyes glazing. Hannigan hit him a third time and the giant released his hold.

The manhunter's heels touched the floor, and he almost went down as he stumbled backwards.

Armir's glassy eyes swept clear and his face flooded with crimson. He started towards the manhunter again.

'Don't!' Hannigan shouted, leveling the Peacemaker. He didn't want to kill an unarmed man but would if it meant his and Tootie's lives.

Armir didn't hesitate. Animal rage clouded his dark eyes. He kept coming forward and Hannigan squeezed the trigger. Thunder exploded in the room, slamming Hannigan's eardrums.

The giant stopped, peered down at

the ripening blossom of scarlet on his chest, then let out an anguished roar and lunged at the manhunter again.

Hannigan triggered another shot. Lead punched into the giant, knocking him backward a step, but halting him not more than an instant. Blood bubbled from Armir's lips and he lumbered towards Hannigan mechanically, driven by pure rage.

The manhunter fired the remaining four shots. Each shot drove the giant backward another step. Armir's movements suddenly lost control, and his limbs took on a strange looseness. His head wobbled and blood streamed from his nostrils and ears.

With a great crash, Armir hit the window and kept going. Glass and frame shattered as the giant went though, arms wind-milling.

A heavy thud sounded from below and Hannigan went to the window, peered down. The giant was sprawled on the street below, arms akimbo, neck twisted at an unnatural angle. He'd bounced off the wooden awning and landed on his head on the hardpack.

Hannigan wiped sweat from his brow, then, shaking, reloaded his gun and slid it back into its holster.

He wasted no time getting down to the lobby. There, he discovered the source of the blood on the giant's knife. It didn't belong to the marshal; it had come from the hotel man, who was sprawled across the counter, throat slit ear to ear. That explained how Armir had gotten Hannigan's room number.

'Christ . . . ' whispered Hannigan, not stopping to examine the man. It was clear he was dead and if Armir hadn't killed the marshal that meant someone else had been dispatched to do the job. It also meant Vago had decided to move against them for some reason.

'Tootie . . . ' he mouthed, throwing open the hotel door and stepping out into the chilly morning air. With a glance at the body of the giant, who was already attracting a few gawkers, he ran along the boardwalk. The marshal's office was on the way to the circus grounds and he wouldn't waste much time there if the lawman already had been murdered.

He stopped just short of the door, pressing against the wall and drawing his Peacemaker again. Peering through the window, he saw Vago's second, Ganado, poised over the lawdog, who lay on the floor. The marshal moved, not dead but obviously incapacitated. Ganado had a knife drawn and poised to plunge it into Wentworth.

Hannigan grabbed the handle and flung open the door.

Ganado whirled from a crouch and sent a dagger flying towards the manhunter.

Hannigan jerked left, half-expecting the move but still surprised Ganado could let fly so quickly from that position with that degree of accuracy.

With a searing welt of pain the dagger shaved off a sliver of his ear, and thudded into the door frame.

Ganado leaped to his feet, whipping a second dagger from a sheath at his waist. Hannigan triggered a shot that punched a hole into the knife-thrower's forehead. Ganado jumped backwards and slammed into the floorboards, unmoving.

Wentworth groaned, struggling to push himself to his feet.

Hannigan holstered his Peacemaker and went to the marshal, hoisting him up and onto the chair in front of his desk.

'You OK?' He peered into the man's eyes. The marshal appeared groggy but unwounded, expect for a small gash on his forehead.

Wentworth nodded. 'He came in here claiming to have some information about what his boss was doing. Like a fool I believed him and when I turned to get him some coffee he tried to put a knife in my back. We struggled and he banged me in the temple with the hilt. Another moment and he would have finished the job.'

Hannigan sighed. 'Vago sent the strongman after me. He's littering your street a few blocks down. I'm going to that circus. If they pulled this stunt Tootie's in trouble and I aim to come down on Vago hard. He'll tell me where that boy is or there won't be enough of him to put in your jail.'

'I'll fetch a deputy and join you.'

'You OK to move?'

The marshal stood, appearing steady enough. 'Hell, yeah, I got a score to settle.'

Hannigan made it out the door before the lawman finished the words.

He ran down the boardwalk, panic invading his mind. The stakes were higher now and if he lost Tootie he lost everything. The thought she might already be dead made his legs nearly buckle, but he forced the notion down, refusing to accept it.

As he approached the circus, he saw movement; clowns and performers were loading wagons, disassembling tents. Most ignored him as he charged onto the grounds, but a few cast him sideways looks. None made a move to get in his way after seeing the wild look in his eyes. He might well have killed anyone who tried to stop him.

Reaching the fortune teller's wagon, he flung open the doors, which crashed into the sides and rebounded. But he'd gotten a good enough look to tell the wagon was empty. His belly sank and his teeth came together hard enough to make balls of muscles stand out on either side of his cheeks.

His gaze jumped to the main tent and his hand went to the ivory grip of his Peacemaker. If Vago had harmed Tootie, Hannigan would put a bullet between his eyes without hesitation or compunction.

He took a step in the direction of the main tent, but a sudden banging stopped him. Eyes narrowing, he peered about, heard the banging come again. His gaze went to the plain wagon near the fortune teller's. Muffled yells came then, from within the wagon. The circus people ignored the sounds, as if they were used to hearing it.

When they'd forced Vago to open that wagon, they'd found it empty, but the manhunter was sure the sounds were coming from within it now.

Hand easing off his gun, he went to the wagon, discovering the padlock back in place.

He banged a fist against the panel. 'Tootie?' he yelled.

A flurry of thudding sounds followed his shout and a surge of relief went through him. She was in there, alive, and that, for the moment, was all he gave a damn about.

Stepping back, he drew his Peacemaker and fired twice at the lock. The padlock practically disintegrated.

He holstered his gun, then snatched the shattered lock from the door and hurled it to the ground. Jerking the doors open, he saw her at the back of the wagon, ankles and hands bound, gagged with a bandana tied about her head.

He leaped into the wagon and went to her, unsheathing his boot knife, then slicing through the ropes. After slipping the blade back into its sheath, he untied the gag, throwing it aside.

She tried to get to her feet, unsteady, almost going down again. He slung an arm about her shoulders, holding her up until the circulation came back to her limbs and she was able to stand on her own.

'Ganado and Vago,' she said and he nodded.

'Ganado's dead. He went after the marshal. Not sure how many of these folk will support Vago when it comes down to it, but I'm going after him — '

'No, Jim!' Tootie grabbed his arm as he started to turn. 'Stay here. I kept hearing noises coming from under the floor of this wagon while I was in here. I'll go after Vago alone.'

'The hell you will — '

'I have to. Please.' Her eyes became pleading and his own narrowed. 'He's my brother.'

'What?' Shock washed across his face. 'Alejandro?'

'He's been alive all this time, changed his name. He's become . . . something inhuman. I have to deal with him myself.'

'I damn well don't like that . . . ' he said, but knew he had no right to deny her request. She pulled a derringer from a skirt pocket.

'They didn't bother to search me.' She gave him a fragile smile then headed for the end of the wagon and jumped out. An instant later she was gone and Hannigan felt every fiber of his being shout at him to go after her.

Her brother. Alejandro del Pelado. Christ, as if thinking he were dead hadn't been hard enough on her . . .

A groan caught his attention and he paused, listening. She had said she heard noises coming from beneath the wagon floor. He jumped out of the wagon and peered under it, not entirely certain what he was searching for. Nothing unusual caught his eye, except maybe for the fact the bottom appeared a little boxier than that of the other wagons. Still, he discovered no odd seams or concealed panels.

He thumped a fist against the side of the wagon and heard a thud in return. Brow cinching, he jumped back into the vehicle and began tapping a boot heel along the floor. A moment later he stopped, as a hollow sound came from the floorboards. He knelt, examining the floor. Fingertips dragging along the boards, he discovered a slight gap running along one of them.

He unsheathed his boot knife and jammed it into the crack, then pried. A panel came up, revealing a compartment beneath the wagon floor. In the compartment he saw a boy, trussed up and gagged, eyes wide with terror. He appeared somewhat groggy and Hannigan reckoned Vago had given him laudanum or some such drug to keep him quiet. But the drug had worn off and in their haste to pull stakes no one had given him another dose.

He sheathed his knife and hauled the child from the compartment, then untied the ropes and removed the gag. He picked up the boy and carried him outside, just as the marshal and another young man were entering the circus grounds, guns drawn.

★ ★ ★

Tootie drew a deep breath before entering the main tent. She had little taste for what she had to do — take in her brother for what would likely result in a hanging when it came out what he had done with those missing kids. She had searched for Alejandro for years, imagined a thousand scenarios as to his fate, her childhood protector. But this monster he'd grown into ... such a possibility had never even remotely entered her thoughts. The notion brought tears to her eyes, a choking sorrow to her soul.

*You have to face it*, she told herself. He had long ago lost hold of his sanity and others had suffered for it. For all intents, the last of her family perished the day Agnes and Harker Pendelton sent her away.

Gripping her nerves, she pushed aside the tent flap and entered, derringer clutched in her bleached hand.

Alejandro del Pelado looked up, a glimmer of shock, then defeat, sparking on his face. 'Since you're here, I suppose that means Hannigan survived and Ganado's dead?'

She nodded, coming deeper into the tent. 'I'm placing you under arrest, Alejandro. You got any sense left in your head you'll tell us what became of those other children and pray God has mercy on your soul.'

He stood, face turning grim. 'It's too late. You'll never find them. And even if I knew where most of them are now I wouldn't tell you. That'd be a sign of weakness, wouldn't it?'

'That'd be a sign there was something human still left in you, Alejandro, something of my brother.'

He laughed, but no humor came with the expression. 'I'm going to walk out the back way, Tootie. You're going to let me go because I'm your brother. I'll ride far away from here and you'll never have to see me again. You can just recollect me as the weak little boy I was, the boy who couldn't stop Agnes and Harker from sending you away.'

'You're wrong, Alejandro. I won't let you do that.'

He smiled. 'Oh, I think you will. After all, you're not strong enough to stop me.'

He moved towards the rear of the tent, turning his back to her, confident she wouldn't stop him. For an instant she wondered if he weren't right. He was her brother. She had searched years to find him. How could she bring him in, knowing what fate awaited him?

'Please, Alejandro, stop. Don't make it worse than it already is.' Her voice shook; she couldn't stop herself. Her derringer came up, hands trembling, aim wavering.

He glanced back. 'Harder on who? Me . . . or you? You always needed protecting, Tootie. You got Hannigan for that, now, far as I can see. But you can't protect yourself. You're still that little girl who fell in the stream and got washed away. Except there's no one to pull you out this time, is there?'

He turned and started to draw back the rear flap. She took a few steps forward.

'Alejandro!' Her voice made him pause only for a second.

A tear slipped down her cheek.

'Goodbye, Tootie . . . ' he said, voice low.

'Please . . . ' she whispered. 'Please don't make me . . . '

He began to step through the opening.

She pulled the trigger.

★   ★   ★

At the sound of the shot, Jim Hannigan grabbed the tent flap and plunged inside. He took in the scene instantly, coming up beside Tootie, who still held her derringer straight-armed, hands shaking, face pinched and wet with tears. Alejandro del Pelado lay on the ground, clutching a wound in his thigh.

'Christ,' Vago mumbled. 'I didn't think you'd . . . '

She lowered the derringer and stepped over to him, peering down. From his eye a frightened boy peered back, any semblance of the control he'd held a few moments before crumbling, a façade erected to hide the tragedy that was the life of Alejandro del Pelado.

'I'm . . . sorry,' she whispered. 'You mistook compassion for weakness.'

'What are you going to do with me, Tootie? Just hand me over?' Spite came with his words now, like a child annoyed that a sibling had tattled.

'You'll get a trial . . . hang likely . . . ' Her words trembled, her body quivered.

'Tootie, have mercy, please. You can tell them I didn't kill anyone directly, put in a good word for me at the trial . . . '

Whatever strength Alejandro del Pelado thought he possessed had now totally deserted him. He appeared nothing more than a coward, an outlaw facing certain justice, a bully unable to stand up to an opponent more powerful than himself.

'You would have killed me, Alejandro. I might have let that slide, same with the robbery. But you consigned those kids to Hell. If we're lucky enough to get any of them back they'll spend their lives dealing with what happened to them. No good words for you . . . '

'But I'm your brother . . . '

She shook her head, then turned away, tears coming again. 'My brother died a long time ago.'

Tootie walked past Hannigan and out into the warming day.

A few moments later the marshal entered the tent, leading the snake charmer, a grim look on his face.

Hannigan glanced at him, then the woman, who looked ready to spit nails.

'I had my deputy take the boy back to his mother. Got a notion he'll stay clear of any carnivals for a spell.'

Hannigan nodded, a dark feeling crawling up inside him at the sight of Vago writhing on the floor, now muttering to himself like a hurt child. 'Find any of the jewels?'

The marshal made a disgusted sound. 'In a manner of speaking. Our snake lady here confessed she forces the snakes to swallow them till they get out of town and can fence them.'

'Christ . . . ' The thought of it made his belly turn.

The marshal grinned. 'Bright side is you stay in Angel Pass the next few weeks there'll be a run on new boots.'

\* \* \*

Three days later found Jim Hannigan and Tootie del Pelado on the trail leading out of Angel Pass. Most of the circus performers were filling the marshal's cells. Some might go free, others would spend a good deal of time in jail on accessory and robbery charges. They'd managed to drag confessions out of a few, leads to the whereabouts of some of the abducted children. The marshal would see to it those leads were followed up. Hannigan would handle a few of them himself. He prayed they would get lucky and find some of the missing children, but knew many would never be located. The men scheduled to be picking up the latest batch would be met by the law and face hard justice.

Alejandro del Pelado would certainly hang.

Hannigan glanced at Tootie in the early morning sunlight. 'You sure you don't want to stay for the trial?'

She shook her head, staring straight ahead. 'No, no point. He ain't my brother anymore. He's some kind of monster.'

He sighed. 'What he became, Tootie ... I don't usually make excuses for men like that but maybe seein' as what your aunt and uncle — '

'No, don't make excuses for him, either, Jim. He made his choices. What happened to him ... was awful but what he became ... was worse.'

Hannigan gripped the reins tighter, knowing she was right but wanting to provide her some measure of comfort. 'Maybe someday what happened to make him that way will let you forgive him a measure ... '

Her face tightened. 'Maybe. Not now. Not for a spell.'

He remained silent a few moments, wishing he was better with words, wishing he was better with emotions.

'You OK?' he asked, gazing over at her.

She gave him a small nod and a lifeless smile. 'Yeah ... I'm all right. Reckon Tooties do float after all ... '

We do hope that you have enjoyed reading this large print book.

Did you know that all of our titles are available for purchase?

We publish a wide range of high quality large print books including:
**Romances, Mysteries, Classics**
**General Fiction**
**Non Fiction and Westerns**

Special interest titles available in large print are:
**The Little Oxford Dictionary**
**Music Book, Song Book**
**Hymn Book, Service Book**

Also available from us courtesy of Oxford University Press:
**Young Readers' Dictionary**
**(large print edition)**
**Young Readers' Thesaurus**
**(large print edition)**

For further information or a free brochure, please contact us at:
**Ulverscroft Large Print Books Ltd.,**
**The Green, Bradgate Road, Anstey,**
**Leicester, LE7 7FU, England.**
**Tel:** (00 44) **0116 236 4325**
**Fax:** (00 44) **0116 234 0205**

## HIGH STAKES AT CASA GRANDE

### T. M. Dolan

A gambler down on his luck, Latigo arrives in town bent on vengeance. His aim is to ruin Major Lonroy Crogan, the owner of the town of Casa Grande, and then to kill him. With a loaned poker stake, he soon makes enough money to threaten Crogan's empire by buying up property. However, danger lurks on the horizon and Latigo's plans seem doomed to failure. Will he be forced to flee Casa Grande as an all round loser?

# SHOWDOWN AT TRINIDAD

## Daniel Rockfern

The big man knew that with no one left who could connect him with the train robbery, he was almost clear. No one, that is, except Frank Angel, special investigator for the US Justice Department. And Hainin realised that there was no stopping the lawman's pursuit. He might get away clear with the money, but Angel would never quit looking for him . . . never forget. It was a pity. But if Hainin was to ever know peace, Angel had to die!

# KID LOBO

## Clayton Nash

He had more than one name but only one reputation that counted: he was the best horse-breaker in West Texas. He knew horses and guns, but he didn't know who his father was. And suddenly it was important to him to find this man who had run out on his mother and left her to work herself to death in her efforts to raise him. He wanted only one thing now: to find that man — and kill him.

# DANGLING NOOSE

## Jack Holt

When Dan Chantry, a struggling farmer, is threatened with fore-closure, a meeting between him and Morgan, his unsympathetic bank manager, turns angry. Chantry vows to stop him should Morgan carry out his threat. Then Morgan is found murdered, and the murder weapon is found in Chantry's saddle-bag. His next stop is the gallows. However he escapes imprisonment, but Al Blake, a friend and marshal of Wolf Creek, captures him. Will Chantry be proved innocent or will he face the gallows?

# SILVER GALORE

## John Dyson

The mysterious southern belle, Careen Langridge, has come West to escape death threats from fanatical Confederates. Is she still being pursued? Should she marry Captain Robbie Randall? The Mexican Artiside Luna has his own plans . . . With gambler and fast-gun Luke Short he murders Randall's men and targets Careen. Can the amiable cowboy Tex Anderson and his pal, Pancho, impose rough justice as with guns blazing they go to Careen's aid?

# CARSON'S REVENGE

## Jim Wilson

When the Mexican bandit General Rodriguez hangs Carson's grandfather, the youngster vows revenge, and with that aim joins the Texas Rangers. Then as Carson escorts Mexican Henrietta Xavier to her home, Rodriguez kidnaps her. The ranger plucks the heiress from the general's clutches, and the youngsters make a desperate run for the border and safety. Will Carson's strength and courage be enough to save them as he tries to get the better of the brutal general and his bandits?